MW01128641

A GHOST OF A CHANCE

BRITTANY KELLEY

A GHOST OF A CHANCE

Published by Brittany Kelley

www.brittanykelleywrites.com

Copyright © 2023 Brittany Kelley

Cover by Okay Creations

Edited by VB Edits

This is a work of fiction. Unless otherwise indicated, all the names, characters, businesses, places, events and incidents in this book are either the product of the author's imagination or used in a fictitious manner. Any resemblance to actual persons, living or dead, or actual events is purely coincidental.

All rights reserved. No portion of this book may be reproduced in any form without permission from the publisher, except as permitted by U.S. copyright law. For permissions contact: admin@brittanykelleywrites.com

For sub-rights inquiries, please contact Jessica Watterson at Sandra Djikstra Literary Agency.

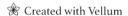 Created with Vellum

This book is for all the misfits—you make a little magic every day.

AUTHOR'S NOTE

Some readers may find themes in this book troubling. For a full list of content warnings, please visit my website.

www.brittanykelleywrites.com

1

Tara

The great thing about small towns is that almost everyone knows each other. On the other hand, the worst thing about small towns is that almost everyone knows each other.

Today, though, it's not necessarily a bad thing.

Smoke curls in sooty clouds from the fiery heap where my downtown business and second-floor apartment once stood, and people I haven't spoken to in years are sending me texts offering casseroles and condolences.

My phone is nearly as hot in my hand as the tears that won't quit running down my cheeks.

A crash sounds as I stand behind the firefighting line, and the sign that read *TAROT, KOLACHE AND TEA* falls to the concrete sidewalk.

Now it blinks *ROT ACHE*, once, then twice, then sends up a shower of sparks before dying... and that pretty much sums up how I feel, too. A big ole rotten ache.

It's muggy and hot and smoke stings my eyes as I watch the

business I built literally fall to the ground. All I can do is watch text after text ding through my phone and five years of hard work go up in smoke and think, *I should have seen it coming.*

Seeing things coming *was* my job, after all.

That's me, fortune teller extraordinaire, renowned throughout New Hopewell, the most haunted town in Texas, according to *Travel and Leisure* magazine, and a complete and total fake.

I probably deserve this for being such a liar. I read the cards, sure, but I also read people. I don't believe in it the way I did when I was starting out.

A firefighter stands in front of me, and I can tell from the way his mouth is moving and the look on his face that he's been talking to me for a few minutes already.

"Sorry, what?" I say, brushing a lock of purple hair out of my eyes.

"I said it looks electrical. The old building caught and just..." He makes an exploding motion with his hands,. "Real lucky you were at the store. You have insurance, right?"

I glance at the brown paper bag on the ground next to me— the ice cream I bought and forgot about is surely completely melted in this late summer heat—and wonder how lucky I am.

"I do. I have insurance." I swallow hard, because now that I'm talking, the tears feel like they're about to overwhelm me and the lump in my throat is so big it hurts.

"Was there anyone inside the building? Pets?"

I shake my head, wrapping my arms around myself. "No. No pets. They already asked me that."

"Of course. Of course. Listen, if I were you, I'd find a place to stay." He jerks his chin at the smoldering rubble. "This kind of thing takes months for insurance to sort out. They'll do an investigation, make sure it wasn't fraud, all that kind of thing. Do you need me to drive you somewhere?"

He gives me a sympathetic look, but the way his gaze drops

to my lips leaves me cold. Is he seriously trying to pick me up? Right now? On this, one of the worst days in my adult life?

I put a hand on my hip, about to say something I might regret later, but as soon as I open my mouth—

"She doesn't need anything else from you, young man," a strong voice rings out, and bony fingers dig into my upper arm. "She's coming home with me."

"Aunt Tilly, what are you doing here?" I swing around, and my aunt smiles back at me, her blue eyes twinkling with mischief.

"Well, I came into town as soon as the New Hopewell phone tree called me. Damn thing's been ringing off the hook."

She holds up her cell phone. It's a brick of a Nokia, the kind I didn't know they even made anymore. When she opens her arms wide for a hug, I don't hesitate.

The acrid smell of smoke disappears and is replaced by her familiar cinnamon-bun and coffee scent. One whiff of Aunt Tilly and the feel of her strong and wiry arms around my chest, and I feel like everything's going to be okay.

I pull back, the urge to cry finally hitting me full force. "Is there really a phone tree? Why didn't I know about it?"

"Your house is on fire, and you're wondering why you didn't know about a phone tree?" She arches a snow-white eyebrow at me. "You know, you're not nearly as upset as I thought you would be."

I don't know what to say to that, so I hug her again.

I am upset.

I am. Of course I am.

"Speaking of the phone tree," Tilly says airily. "Has Sarah Hodgins called you? Her goulash is my favorite. You know what?" She tugs my phone out of my hand, then casually holds it up to my face, unlocking it. "I'll take care of that."

"What?" I sputter, but Aunt Tilly's already using my phone, ignoring me completely.

"Hi, Sarah. Hi hon. Yes, that's why I was calling." She winks at me, then affixes her face into a solemn frown that looks wildly out of place. "Just horrible. The poor thing is in shock. Can't even manage to cry. Oh yes." She pauses, narrowing her eyes at me critically. "She does. She looks horrible."

I gape, then look down at myself. Sure, I'm not dressed to impress, but I love this little black jumpsuit. I love my graphic tee under it, too.

"Honestly, I'll have to take her shopping. A whole new wardrobe. Of course! Yes, she's staying with me. For however long it takes to get her back on her feet."

She laughs at something Sarah says, and I can't do more than stare as heat washes over my face. From the fire, yes, but also... maybe a little bit from embarrassment, too.

"Yes, of course we want the goulash. I'll have my hands full with trying to sort her out and keeping up with that old house, you know?"

She's silent for a moment, and I pluck at my jumpsuit, frowning harder. Sort me out? What is that supposed to mean?

"Oh yes, we would love an extra pan of it. That would be so generous of you. Mm-hmm. No, we're not dairy free. So sweet of you to ask. And I tell you what, will you tell the rest of the girls that we could use a hand? The more meals we have—she has—the easier it will be on her. She needs things to be easy right now, the poor dear." She nods, then smacks me in the thigh, a celebratory swing that stings. "Yes, we love the chicken tetrazzini, and the Caesar salad. Of course, anything is welcome. You know, I'm sure some of your famous sourdough bread would lift her spirits. Five loaves is probably just right, uh-huh. Of course. No, thank you. You are an angel. Oh, I have to go. She's just started crying."

Aunt Tilly hangs up on poor Sarah Hodgins, who she's just managed to dupe into sending her a week's worth of food, along with, if she can convince the rest of the New Hopewell ladies, probably an additional month or two's worth.

I'm not even mad. I'm impressed. And a little terrified.

I swallow hard, and she grins at me like the Cheshire Cat. A white-haired one, but just as unpredictable.

"What's it going to cost me to come stay with you, Aunt Tilly?"

"Oh, please. Pish-posh." She waves a hand, her aqua-painted nails sparkling in the late September sunshine. "Not much. Not at all."

"Aunt Tilly," I say, trying to inject as much warning as I can into my voice.

"I'll tell you about it when you get in the car," she cajoles, fluttering her eyelashes.

"Nuh-uh." I shake my head, because if I know my Aunt Tilly, she's working an angle. Not that she's not generous—she's a great person. She was always my confidant at the rare family get-togethers. The black sheep aunt I couldn't wait to spend time with. "Tell me now."

As much as love Tilly, I'm not an idiot, and I pride myself on being able to read people.

She sighs, patting at her short white hair. "It's not much. Not for someone like you."

I peer at her, slightly concerned about what the heck that's supposed to mean. Her ancient Volvo sits in a corner spot, gleaming in the bright September sun. The scratch on the side door from when she taught me how to drive it has long since been repaired, but I imagine if I slanted my head at it just right, I could still see it.

When we climb inside, the old leather seats creak. They're still supple enough but starting to show their age.

"You forgot your groceries," she tells me, starting up the car. It takes a few tries before the engine turns over, and Aunt Tilly pats the dash lovingly.

I snort. "I think you've got enough food coming for the rest of the year."

"Not hardly." She winks at me, grinning, then throws the car into reverse and rests her aged hand against the back of my seat as she carefully backs up.

I lean my head back against the headrest, assaulted by memories flashing through me as I inhale the scent of leather conditioner and caramel, thanks to the lifetime supply of inexplicable caramel-flavored car deodorizers Tilly bought on sale one Black Friday years and years ago.

We're on the pine-lined highway, the only sound the blasting of the air conditioner, before I remember the strings Tilly's prepared to use to manipulate me like a merry marionette.

"Tell me what it is you want me to do for you, Aunt Tilly," I say quietly, watching her out of the corner of my eye.

A muscle tightens at her temple before she glances over and grins at me.

Interesting.

"Well, an old woman like me can't be expected to do all the work on a house and property like our family estate by herself."

"That's all?" I ask, surprised. "Of course. I don't mind helping out however I can—"

"And I need you to get rid of the ghosts." She says it so matter-of-factly that it takes me a minute to process the absurdity of her words.

I huff a laugh, and that muscle twitches in her temple again.

"I don't believe in ghosts," I tell her. "So I'd be happy to help you get rid of the non-existent bogeymen. First off, I'll call that firefighter and have him check for carbon monoxide."

Tilly manages to give me a withering look while driving, a feat that makes me feel like I'm thirteen again and have been shipped off to stay with her again so my parents can have their child-free summer. She softens it with a quiet, musical laugh that softens the memory, though, and I impulsively reach over and squeeze her wrist affectionately.

It's bonier than I remember, less substantial, and her skin is paper-thin against my palm.

"You don't remember all our holidays communing with the spirits?" Tilly asks archly.

"Of course I do." I settle my hand back in my lap, watching the evergreens laden with pinecones race by outside the window. "You gave me a skill set that I grew into a business."

Tilly taught me tarot. She taught me to be open-minded. She taught me little witchy rituals that made me feel special and close to her. She taught me how to be... well, *me*.

But... I grew up. I brushed off a lot of what we did those summers and fall breaks and winter vacations as imaginary.

A prickle goes down my back.

I thought Tilly did it to keep me entertained. To keep us both entertained.

I narrow my eyes, examining her closely. Sure, she's gotten older, as I have too, and I see hints of myself in her strong nose and high cheekbones, but... what if she's not—

"Do not even think about looking at me like that, young lady," she barks, startling me.

"Like what?"

"Like I've lost my marbles. You might not want to believe that the supernatural exists, but trust me, Tara, they believe in you."

I swallow hard. "I'll help you with the ghosts," I tell her meekly.

"And you can help me with my neighbor."

My nose wrinkles. "Neighbor? I thought that old place was abandoned."

She inhales deeply, her nostrils flaring white with outrage. "It was. The Carlisles wised up and moved out decades ago, only for their awful heir to move in and start restoring the place."

"God forbid it be restored," I mutter under my breath.

"My thoughts exactly!" she screeches.

Her signal chimes loudly as we exit the highway to the rural two-lane farm road that leads to her amazing Victorian-style manor and acres of gorgeous wooded land.

I sigh, relaxing in my seat.

Maybe staying with Aunt Tilly is just what I need.

The dense tangle of East Texas forest I remember suddenly gives way to an open expanse of manicured lawn and precisely placed firecracker salvia buzzing with bees. I sit up straight, my jaw dropping at the bright white picket fence running alongside the road.

I don't remember *this*.

A tall man, well over six feet, stands next to an unfinished trellis gate, a shovel in hand.

And no shirt on.

Miles of abs. Miles of them. And then a sharp vee leading into his pants.

My mouth snaps shut, barely keeping the drool from escaping.

"Does he work for your neighbor?" I ask, fanning my face. "You could hire him, too."

Sweat glides down his body, and I lick my lips. His face is shadowed by the baseball cap on his head, but if it matches that body? Whew.

"That's Ward Carlisle," Aunt Tilly snarls. "The devil himself."

"Hot," I manage.

Aunt Tilly arches an eyebrow at me.

"In hell," I add belatedly. "Must be hot in hell. Where the devil lives."

"You watch out for him, Tara. Looks can be deceiving."

"Mm-hmm," I say. If Aunt Tilly thinks he's good-looking enough to be deceiving, then his face is probably just as fine as the rest of him.

Whew.

Before long, we're turning onto Tilly's property—our family's historic home—and I frown at what greets me.

Overgrown beds, weeds trailing over the once well-kept willow branch fencing—Tilly's pride and joy. I helped her construct half of them one fall after she special-ordered the branches from a state up north that actually grows the type of willow we needed. I came away from that project with a newfound appreciation for a good pair of gardening gloves and more splinters than I cared to count.

What used to be a proliferation of late summer and early fall blooms has fallen into complete chaos. I swallow hard.

"Don't you dare say a word, missy," Tilly tells me. "I haven't seen you volunteering to come help out like you used to. Or even come by for dinner."

Guilt swamps me, and I bite back the defensiveness that threatens on its heels.

"You're right," I say instead. "I'm sorry. I haven't... I was busy with the store, and just trying to—"

I cut myself off, stopping myself from saying the words that I've kept inside for a couple of years.

Trying to keep afloat.

Trying not to drown in the well of debt I've been clawing my way out of since starting up an... unlikely business in the Bible Belt.

"Well, I can't say that I thought you would actually apologize." She harrumphs, and I bite my cheek, trying not to grin at her flustered response. "Maybe you've done more growing up than I give you credit for."

I can't help but look at her askance. I'm thirty-two. I'm very much an adult, and have all the... well, shit.

Maybe I don't have anything to prove it.

My business is gone.

I don't have a significant other.

I barely make time to see my other friends in town, though they're all busy, too.

And now I'm moving in with my elderly aunt.

"Maybe. Maybe not," I shrug one shoulder.

"As long as you haven't gotten too big for your britches to help me out around here, then we'll be just fine."

"I would love to help you. It's the least I can do. At least I won't have to cook for us," I tell her, and she grins at me. Gravel drive gives way to asphalt as we get closer to the house, and I clutch at my purse, staring up at the out-of-place Victorian manor. It captivated me as a child, the gabled roofs and turret with bay windows out front. The porch is as picturesque as I remember, wrapping around the front of the house. The fans spinning lazily overhead are not quite up to historic standards, but Aunt Tilly never gave two shits about that.

In the relentless Texas heat, I can't say I blame her.

Virginia creeper climbs up the side of the slate blue siding, clinging to white shutters and cedar shake, green leaves shuddering in some phantom breeze. I follow it up and up, all the way to the third-story attic, where something stirs in the window.

I swallow hard, ignoring the cold chill of fear that grips me right between my shoulder blades.

"The old girl doesn't look half-bad, does she?"

"That creeper is going to ruin the siding," I make myself say.

"Nah, it adds character. If you're going to live in a haunted house, you may as well make it look the part."

"You're just saying that because you haven't been able to get it off."

"Absolutely," Tilly agrees. "But I gotta give the bunko ladies something to chat about, right? The ghosts love it, too."

Tilly maneuvers the boat of a car around the exterior of the house, and smooth drive gives way to crunching gravel once again as we make our way to the east side of her property.

"The willow's huge."

"Has it really been that long since you've been here?" She peers at me, but there's no censure in the question. Just mild surprise.

I do some mental math. "Five years, probably."

"Some niece I have," she says. "Can't even be bothered to come visit once in five years."

"Aunt Tilly, it's not like you haven't seen me," I argue, knowing that it's a lost cause. She's right, anyway.

"Brunch every other month hardly counts as a satisfactory visit."

"All the kolaches and lattes I gave you on the house beg to differ."

"Not my fault you're not a great saleswoman."

I snort at that. "I could hardly charge my wonderful, beautiful, generous Aunt Tilly for brunch."

"I know that's right," she agrees, grinning at me.

Slowly, she angles the car up another overgrown path, where the gravel gives way to hard-packed dirt. Clouds of dust cough up around the windows, and then we're in the shade of a massive live oak tree. Spanish moss drips from the branches, pale green and likely full of bugs.

"Remember that time Lettie got stuck up there, so you went to get her, and then you got stuck too?"

"That cat was a menace," I tell her, peering up into the thick branches.

"Lettie was a sweetheart."

"Sure," I tell her. "An escape artist and a vermin serial killer with razor-sharp claws and a heart of gold."

"You can't blame her for acting like a cat," Tilly says, putting the car in park.

I laugh, an ache settling around my chest. I've missed Tilly. I let the stupid café and shop take over my life, and for what? To watch it burn down, with nothing to show for all the years of hard work I scraped away at.

"The ghosts wanted you to come," Tilly says, staring at me with wide blue eyes.

I startle, swallowing past the lump in my throat.

"For someone who doesn't believe in them, you sure look pale, honey."

"You said that just to get me to stop crying," I accuse.

"Diversion is an excellent tactic," Tilly tells me merrily. "You ready to take a look at your guest house? I had it fixed up last year. Of course, the only ones who have stayed in it have been dust bunnies and daddy longlegs. Somebody has been too busy to come stay."

"I wouldn't have even stayed out here if I came over. I would have stayed in the main house." Disbelief wrinkles my forehead, and I stare at her for a minute. "You can't be serious right now."

Annoyed with her and with myself for being annoyed with her, I open the door, and the September Texas heat hits me like a shovel to the face.

The little guest house is completely different from the Victorian just barely visible down the way. The casita style architecture is adorable in its own right, and Tilly looks to have spared no expense on restoring it to its former glory. Tan stucco walls and red tiles look cozy nestled among the live oaks and silvery sage.

I put a hand over my eyes, staring in disbelief at a sign on the front door.

"Tilly... is that a neon dick? You put a neon dick on the front door?"

A long-suffering sigh escapes her mouth, and she shuts the

car door, standing beside me as we both tilt our heads, taking in the dick on the door.

"I got a great deal on it," she says, and I raise my eyebrows at her. "I've never been able to pass up a deal on dick."

I choke on an inhalation. "I don't even..."

"You're going to love the inside," she trills, and I follow her in, full of much more trepidation than I was on our way here.

One look at the inside tells me I was right to be worried.

2

Ward

My asshole of a neighbor has another group of bachelorettes in her car. I'm positive. One look at the pretty raven-haired woman next to her as she drove by, gleefully smiling, and I know I'm in for another raucous week of drunk women screaming strange requests at me.

Fuck. I throw the shovel down, hot and bothered in all the worst ways.

Mostly just fucking hot, because it's like Texas hasn't gotten the memo that the last few days of September shouldn't feel like a front-row seat to Satan's armpit.

The temperature is ridiculous, and I know my temper is, too, but I'm sick and tired of this Tilly woman torturing me with drunk bachelorettes intent on making my life even more of a living hell.

I grit my teeth, tossing my gloves on top of my shovel, and decide it's time to finally have some choice words with my neighbor.

Which words, I don't know, but I'll figure out something appropriate on the short walk to the little casita that butts up against my property... along with the bevy of wine-drunk women that rent out the party-themed property every weekend, managing to keep me up with their shenanigans.

"Can't keep doing this," I growl under my breath, sweat dripping between my shoulder blades. "Want a show? I'll give them a show."

Dappled shade provides momentary relief from the broiling sun, and a chill goes over me as I pass across the invisible line that separates our two properties. Tilly, who seemed perfectly normal and kind the first time we met, has turned out to be the absolute bane of my existence, doing everything in her power—and by the power vested in bachelorette parties determined to torment me—to drive me out of my house.

And to buy this strip of property that's been contested between our families for generations, or so she says.

I haven't lived here. Not until a couple years ago, when I inherited the property and decided I'd had enough of the big city for one lifetime.

I envisioned chickens, maybe goats. Spending time planting vegetables and pulling weeds and working remote. Maybe even, god forbid, making friends in this tiny town.

What I've gotten, though, is a year or so of peace, a surplus of tomatoes, and then the past eight months of complete and utter chaos, thanks to Tilly's underhanded scheme to drive me off my land.

Vis-à-vis the clientele her little rental property caters to.

Of course, none of this is entirely provable, but I can't imagine she's not behind it.

"She's a wily one," I mutter, finally tromping onto her property, the red-roofed casita in view now. I move faster beneath the shade of the towering live oaks, determined to finally have the last word with Tilly.

The door of the little rental house is ajar, and I don't bother knocking. I'm fed the fuck up of being polite.

Not that I've actually been especially polite.

Turns out the small Southern niceties that are a specialty of small-town Texas never quite made it into my vocabulary.

AC hits my bare skin like an ice bucket, and then I stop entirely, brought up short by an overwhelming sense of shock.

It's like I walked into a hot pink bottle of Pepto Bismol, which, judging by the fully stocked bar in the living room, anyone staying in this place might need, too.

Every wall is pink. Not pretty, pale, girly pink, but the most aggressive shade of pink I've ever laid eyes on. The entire place is an assault on the senses, from the wall of fur boas proclaiming *take me!* to a shelf lined with dildos in sizes and shapes I had no idea they even made. A sign over the sex toy shelf screams *don't be a stranger!*

A disco ball casts rainbows onto it, and I can't stop staring.

"Is that glitter? That whole wall?" a musical voice asks, the questions echoing the same disbelief I feel deep in my bones.

I finally manage to tear my gaze away from the confusing and, frankly, disturbing collection of silicone oddities to find Tilly watching me with a gleeful expression from where she stands beside a young-ish woman with dark, dark brown hair with a decidedly exasperated cast to her lips.

"It is glitter," Tilly answers her. "I see you admiring my monster dildo collection," she tells me sweetly. "I have one that deposits eggs up there, if you want to take it home."

I blink.

"She is not allowed to stay here," I say, whatever speech I'd mentally rehearsed on my angry jaunt to Tilly's den of iniquity disappearing from my brain. "I've had enough of you hosting wild parties. I haven't slept in months."

"Oh no, that is such a tragedy," Tilly says, her smirk telling me everything I need to know.

The other woman, who, even though lit by bright pink walls, neon lights, and disco ball rainbows, is stunningly pretty, looks between us with a slightly dazed expression.

I can't say I blame her.

This place is enough to kill all my brain cells in one go. No wonder the women's weekends quickly devolve into alcohol-fueled sprints through my property and skinny dips in the pond behind my house.

"You should go home," I tell her. "You don't want your bachelorette party or girls' weekend or whatever the fuck you have planned here." I gesture to the wall full of sex toys. "Surely your soon-to-be husband or wife or whomever wouldn't want whatever... whatever this leads to."

She tilts her head at me, stripes of purple flashing under the brown. "My whomever?"

"Yeah, you know, whatever it is you're here to celebrate. It's a bad fucking idea." Another shiny object catches my eye, and I swallow. "Is that a stripper pole?"

"Sure is. Why? You want to take it for a spin?" Tilly asks innocently. "My weekenders love it."

I bet they do.

I scratch at my jaw, then point at the brunette. The more I look at her, the more I like what I see. Dark lashes fringe chocolate brown eyes. Her mouth is full and painted wine-red. Her body is deliciously curved... her nose, though. I squint. There's something familiar about her nose.

"My niece will be staying here for as long as she needs to, Ward Carlisle," Tilly tells me. "Her home just burned down. What kind of a man suggests turning her out on the street after that, huh? Not a good one, I can tell you that. I guess the kind that barges into someone else's guest house half-naked and making wild accusations."

I blink. Her niece. I stare. I blink again.

"She's not here for a bachelorette party? She's not getting

married and having one last girls' weekend?" I ask, some of the wind going out of my sails.

"Nope," the woman answers. "My name's Tara. Not getting married." She holds out a hand. Her nails are painted a bright purple. "And I don't plan on hosting any wild parties."

I start to take her hand, relieved to hear she's not getting married... I mean, uh, that she's not here for a wild weekend designed to drive me insane.

"My hands are dirty," I tell her brusquely. "I've been garden-ing." I glower at Tilly. "Unlike some people."

"I don't answer to you, Ward Carlisle," Tilly says airily. "I can keep my garden however I want."

"I'll be helping her with that," Tara says, glancing between us with narrowed eyes.

My brain is still trying to catch up to the fact that I might actually get a few peaceful nights when my eyes snag on a hand-lettered sign sprinkled with rhinestones.

Tilly steps in front of it. "Now, now, Ward. No reason to get bent out of shape."

"Move." The demand comes out on a low warning note that surprises us both.

"Ward, I—"

"I said *move*, Tilly."

Pain spikes through my head as I clench my jaw and I fist my hands at my sides as I read the sign that takes up most of the wall. Fucking hell. Fucking *hell*.

"Aunt Tilly? What is that?" Tara asks, a mixture of amuse-ment and something else I can't be bothered with determining.

"I fucking knew it," I grind out, beyond angry. Livid.

"Tilly's House Bucket List," Tara reads out loud.

- Get drunk on margaritas (complimentary!)
- Do a magic spell (check the kitchen cupboard for ingredients and spell directions!)

- Run naked through the woods
- Skinny dip in the pond by moonlight
- Sing at the stars at 2 AM
- Morning mimosas starting at 4 AM (complimentary!)
- Karaoke with the roosters at 5 AM

"I FUCKING KNEW you were doing this on purpose," I snarl, hardly recognizing my voice. "I fucking *knew* it. That's my pond they've been skinny-dipping in. Those are my woods. And that is my time to sleep when they've been fucking singing." I manage not to shout at her, even though I want to, but fury leaves me breathless.

Both women stare at me with matching wide eyes.

"This is why sleep deprivation is used as a torture tactic," I finally say. "You... you..." I can't find the words, so I just shake my finger at Tilly, who somehow manages to keep a straight face.

With one last angry shake of my finger, I march out of the hellish pink house.

"Nice to meet you," Tara manages to call out right before I slam the door shut.

"Fuck off," I yell back.

I'm going to take a fucking nap. That way, if Tara or Tilly or who-the-fuck-ever decides to go skinny-dipping in my goddamn pond, I'll be awake enough to tell her to get the hell off my property.

Visions of Tara skinny-dipping in my pond are the last thing I need to be thinking about as I storm back to my house.

3

Tara

Aunt Tilly didn't have much to say for herself after Ward told us to fuck off, but I don't think I was imagining the self-satisfied look on her face as she told me to be up at the house in a couple of hours for dinner.

I can't say I even blame Ward.

What the hell is Aunt Tilly thinking with this shit? I'm no lawyer, but what she's doing seems like harassment. It doesn't sit right with me, that's for sure.

I frown at the wall o' dildos. Now that the sun's going down, I'm pretty sure a few of them are emitting a faint glow.

Can't say I love the décor choice, even though I do admire Tilly's literal balls-to-the-wall execution of a theme.

I sigh, rubbing my forehead and trying to figure out what the hell kind of day I've had.

Store and home burned down? Check.

Moved into an inexplicably flamingo pink and dick-themed house? Check.

Was told to fuck off by a seriously angry and sexy shirtless man? Check.

Could actually fuck off thanks to the silicone monster cocks glowing faintly in the dusk? Absolutely.

Feels like a hygiene issue, though. My lip curls in disgust, and I bark a laugh.

"What the fuck?" I ask nobody.

My phone's charging on the counter, thanks to Aunt Tilly's box of chargers for whoever she's renting the place to, and my phone seems like a good place to start figuring out what exactly the fuck I'm supposed to do next.

One glance at the screen shows about a jillion missed texts and calls, which warms my heart as well as drives home my new glitter-walled reality.

This really happened.

"It really happened," I say out loud. I'm allowed to talk to myself after the freak show of a day I've had.

The glittery black chandelier that lights the kitchen sways slightly, and then the lights blink on and off just as rapidly. I sigh.

"Please. The last thing I need is an electrical fire here. It's like I'm cursed," I mutter.

The lights blink on and off again, and I frown at the garish light fixture. I mean, there isn't anything really wrong with it, but it's not quite my taste. Tilly certainly knows how to commit to a bit.

I peer at the fixture. One of the bulbs looks loose.

A chair scratches across the laminate floor as I pull it out, carefully climbing onto it to screw the bulb in the entire way.

The chandelier turns on.

"There we go," I say, feeling accomplished.

Until I hop off the chair and look back at my phone. It's lit up with messages from people I should probably respond to.

Ugh. Maybe tomorrow.

I scroll through it for a moment, and a voicemail from Emma, who's grown to be my closest friend over the past year or so she's lived here, stops me short.

"Holy shit. What the fuck, Tara? I heard your place burned down, but I didn't believe it until I drove by tonight. Are you okay? I have a guest bed at my house if you want to crash there for a few days. My sister is coming into town next week, but she can sleep on the couch. Please let me know what I can do. If you don't, I swear to god I'll hunt you down and torture you into giving me all the gory details over gelato or margaritas or whatever you're in the mood for."

The message ends, and I smile soggily at the chandelier.

"She's a good friend," I tell it.

A vibration startles me, and I jump, nearly whacking my arm into the countertop. Pink quartz, I think.

It's not my phone, though, and I look around wildly, trying to figure out where it's coming from. That's when one of the monster-dong dildos shakes right off the shelf.

It hits the ground in a glittering purple silicone coup de grâce, then writhes for a few moments before turning off.

Cold swirls around my ankles. It's probably the AC kicking on, though the unit seems silent.

I shiver, unsettled.

Unsettled by a haunted sex toy. Yes. Absolutely.

"Fuck this," I shout at the offending phantom cock. "You're going in a box."

I pause, taking a second to unpack that statement. "A cardboard box," I clarify.

Yes. I don't have the energy to go through all the texts and voicemails piling up on my phone, but I do have the energy to make this space less... well, whatever it is.

I march to the laundry room, which, despite being exactly where I remember it, looks completely different.

YOU LOOK GOOD NAKED! a neon pink sign yells at me from above the washer and dryer.

"It's a lot of word art for me," I mumble, grabbing the (pink!) laundry basket and jetting off to the living room.

I put the basket beneath the shelves, then stare at the purple dildo for a minute.

I glance at the shelf full of dildos.

My lip curls.

"Nope," I say, shaking my head and pulling the eggplant-printed fleece blanket off the couch and wrapping it around my hands like the sex toys might jump off and bite me if they touch my skin.

If one of them lays eggs, maybe one of them bites. Who knows?

I don't want to find out.

One by one, the dildos wiggle their way into the laundry basket, liberated from the bizarre display on the wall.

"Okay then... Just gotta find a new home for all of y'all," I tell the silicone staring up at me forlornly. Too forlornly. I throw the eggplant blanket over them.

Anthropomorphizing monster dildos seems like a slippery slope. Better to not look at them at all.

I heft the surprisingly heavy basket into my arms, gritting my teeth and casting my gaze around the bachelorette dream-house until I decide that the best place for these... *things* is probably in a closet somewhere.

Good grief.

I haven't even looked in the bedrooms of this place yet. What glittering pink horrors await me there?

Grunting, I kick one of the bedroom doors open, prepared for the worst, only to find the room painted a serene blue, with white fluffy clouds stenciled all over.

"Huh." I stare for a minute, transfixed by the space. It's so totally different from the rest of the house. All the furniture is white, and so is the bedding. Two spherical lamps click on as I walk by them, casting a warm glow through the room.

This isn't bad. A little kitschy and too themed for me, but not—

A sign over the bed blinks to life, and I sigh as I read it.

Mile High Club.

Well, that explains the clouds. I snort, managing to toe the closet door open. There. There's just enough room for the haunted dildos in the corner if I move the basket full of spare linens out of the way.

It takes me another few minutes to decide not to pop the Mile High Club sign off the wall, seeing as how the closet is now stuffed to the hilt with dildos.

There's a phrase I never thought I'd use.

A quick perusal of the other two tiny rooms quickly proves the Mile High Club is my best option. The Dracula themed room is a bit too fifty shades of red for me, and the room painted to look like an actual dungeon might give me nightmares.

Besides, the Mile High Club boasts the biggest bed—a king, I think.

I'll take the weird signage for a chance to sprawl like a starfish across it.

I open the bathroom door, prepared for the worst, but it looks totally normal, mostly untouched, and I thank whatever contractor put their foot down about god knows what tile choices Tilly planned on.

Okay.

That's a few things off the to-do list. I know where I'm sleeping, and the sex toys are settling into their new closet corner.

Dark is falling outside. The relative quickness of sunset is the only clue that Texas is moving into fall, heat be damned. It's barely seven o'clock, and I'd usually have a whole host of tasks to do to get ready for the next day of work, but now?

I don't even have my laptop.

Or clothes.

Or... anything.

I don't know what to do besides worry, so I take a quick shower (with complimentary champagne-and-strawberry body wash). There's a huge T-shirt (complimentary) that has the name of Tilly's rental property scrawled across it, and like everything else, it's written in screaming neon.

It smells clean and like the lavender sachets lining the drawer.

I open the rest of the drawers, sniffing at the hot pink tulle bag.

Not just lavender. Not if I know my herbs. Which I do, because Tilly taught me everything she knows about gardening and small magics, and these aren't regular drawer sachets. Nope.

These smell like rose and bay leaves and marigolds, and these aren't for scent. Not at all.

Goose bumps pebble across my arms and a chill runs down my spine. Somewhere in the living room, a floorboard creaks, and I go still.

These are protection sachets—little bags of herbs made to keep bad... whatever away. Ghosts, if Tilly actually believes what she told me. Evil spirits.

I open all the drawers in the room.

There are hundreds of them.

Hundreds.

With the drawers all open, the faint lavender and rose scent I barely noticed earlier is overpowering.

Tilly must have made these. Whatever she thinks is out here, she's legitimately concerned.

My Aunt Tilly doesn't scare easy.

I don't believe in this shit... but she does.

I swallow hard.

The sound of the doorknob turning makes my blood run cold, and I freeze in place, a purple tulle sachet in hand.

Yeah, that's the weapon I want in case of an intruder.

Dried herbs. Perfect.

The door opens, and I steel myself for whoever—whatever —is on the other side.

No one is there.

I blow out a breath. No one is in the hallway, either. I look both ways, just in case, still holding the purple pouch in front of me. For what rational reason, I couldn't tell you.

I guess the little lavender and rose petal concoction makes me feel protected, at the very least.

I turn the corner into the living room and can't help the piercing shriek that comes out of me. The pouch leaves my hands like a possessed baseball.

Tilly stands in the middle of the room, gaping at me, green mask all over her face. "Why are you yelling at me? I should be yelling at you after the way you dismantled my collection."

"Sorry," I say, putting a hand to my chest and inhaling deeply, attempting to calm my galloping heart.

"You threw my own protection spell at me," she adds, highly affronted underneath the sage-colored clay. "What did you think it would do?"

"It was a reflex," I say, putting my hands on my bare knees. The T-shirt doesn't cover quite that far, unfortunately. "I'm jumpy, that's all."

And half-naked out in the woods, I nearly say, but since it seems like Tilly is encouraging that sort of thing, I don't think she'd care.

"Why are you carrying it around?" She peers at me, concern cracking the mask drying on her forehead. "Did you see something?"

"Nope. Not one thing," I answer brightly.

"Uh-huh. Sure."

"All I saw was a bunch of dried floral arrangements," I tell her sharply.

She gives me a long look. "For someone who sells the same shit in her burnt-down shop, you sure sound judgy. At least I'm not trying to make money off a craft I don't even believe."

I inhale, slightly wounded, because she's not wrong.

"I thought you didn't believe in this," she adds, picking up the pouch.

"Is it time for dinner?" I ask. "I'm starving. I don't think I ate lunch. I'm pretty sure I left it on the sidewalk by my shop." My throat closes up, and my heart rate picks up for a new reason.

Stress.

God, I need to call insurance. I need to call the fire department and file reports or whatever. This is a whole damn mess.

My distress must be clear, because Aunt Tilly makes a reassuring clucking sound, like a clay-covered mother hen, and tucks me into her side.

"Don't you worry. I'll help you figure it out, okay? Let's get some food in you, and I'll pack you a little overnight bag for out here. Some spare toiletries, and maybe you can borrow some of my flip-flops. I might have gone a little crazy at the Croc outlet..."

She continues prattling at me, pushing me out the door and into the balmy night air, where her car waits in the drive.

The hair raises on the back of my neck, standing at full attention, and more goose bumps prickle all over my skin.

Something is watching us. I can feel it, sure as the stars twinkling in the Texas night sky overhead. That sixth sense of awareness makes me stand completely still.

Tilly stops, too, her babble cutting off as we both look behind us.

There's nothing there.

"Tilly." My voice cracks on her name. "Let's get in the car, yes?"

I don't have to ask twice. We both scramble into her Volvo, and the engine sputters to life as she tears back in reverse.

We're silent the whole drive to her old Victorian.

"Why can't I stay with you here?" I ask her, feeling stupid and plaintive and silly for being scared. She's rubbing off on me, just like my mom always said she did. And my mom definitely didn't mean it in a nice way.

"I had a pipe burst." Her voice is hoarse, her hands trembling on the wheel as she turns the car off. The headlights die on the drive, and darkness pulls tight as a winter blanket around us. "Several. All but my room is molding while I wait for the plumber and construction crew to come around. I sent off most of the antique furniture, including the beds, to a specialist so they can restore it from all the water damage... I would put you on the couch, but I sincerely thought you'd be more comfortable out there." Her voice warbles, and she sounds like she's on the verge of tears.

It's too damn dark out here to tell whether she's really about to cry, but I never could stand crying. And Tilly? Tilly is too strong to cry.

I pat her wrist. "It's fine, Tilly. Don't worry about it. I don't want to put you out. I'll stay out... there."

A lump forms in my throat, and for the first time today, it's not from swallowing tears.

It's fear.

"Come on," I hear myself say, feeling a mile away from my body. "Let's eat some tetrazzini—"

"King ranch casserole," she interrupts, wiping her eyes. "Sleep with some of those sachets in bed with you, okay?" She squeezes my wrist. "You'll be fine."

"I will," I agree with a smile.

It sounds like we're both lying.

4

Ward

Singing floats through the open windows of the old house. I've got several fans on, because along with all the myriad of other problems I inherited, the electrical wiring needs to be upgraded before I can replace the AC.

All these thoughts fly through my head before I open my eyes. Pure rage brought on by chronic sleep deprivation and the heat makes me feel half out of my mind. A small part of me insists that I should just shut the window and get back in bed, but that little whisper of a voice is completely drowned out by the singing outside my window.

A light bobs in the strip of land between Tilly's property and mine, and before I'm even fully awake, I'm putting shoes on and half out the door, ready to give whoever the hell is out there a piece of my mind.

Or two pieces. However many fucking pieces it takes.

The air is heavy with moisture, and humidity blankets the ground with a thick, low-lying fog. It swirls around my ankles as I walk. The flip-flops I barely remember putting on slap against the soles of my feet.

It's pitch-black out. Clouds obscure the stars, and with the fog playing tricks on me, I belatedly wonder why I didn't grab my flashlight, or, at the very least, my phone.

The singing grows louder, though, and I follow it, letting my acidic rage at being woken up again dissolve any sense of good reason. Can't let things like logic get in the way.

"Enough," I finally boom, and the woman singing, wearing a strange, old-fashioned dress, stares at me with wide, dark eyes. "I am sick and tired of being woken up at this god-forsaken hour. I don't care what Tilly's—"

Mist curls around the woman, and when I blink, she's gone.

Gone.

A chill runs down my spine, and a strange, overwhelming urge to run grips me.

"What in the cottagecore fuck was that bitch wearing?" a sleepy voice asks, and I nearly jump out of my skin. "Did she wake you up too?"

I turn slowly, half-afraid that the singing woman is going to be at my elbow and half-aware that whatever the thing was that was singing, it wasn't a woman at all.

But all I find is Tara.

She's rumpled with sleep. Her dark brown- and purple-streaked hair hangs in loose waves around her shoulders and a huge T-shirt hangs off one shoulder.

"Pussy... palace?" I read, nonplussed at everything that's just happened.

"Apparently, that's what my aunt calls her vacation rental. Charming, right?" She yawns and covers her mouth with one hand. She's got something purple dangling from it, but in the dark, it's hard to make out what it is.

I stare at her for a second, trying to make sense of every-thing I've just seen.

"That was a weird outfit, right? Like, if you're going to wake me up dressed as a historical reenactor and singing, you might as well bring me some fresh-churned butter."

"This is a prank," I tell her slowly, my brain coming to the only conclusion that makes sense. "Your aunt... she hasn't been shy about telling me she thinks this land is your family's. She's trying to make me move, isn't she?"

"Aunt Tilly?" Tara pushes a lock of shining hair out of her face, the little purple bag waving in her hand.

"Why are you holding... what's the word? Potpourri?"

"Oh." She looks at the bag, then up at me with big brown eyes. "It was under my pillow, and I just grabbed it. You think Aunt Tilly is pranking us?" There's a fair amount of skepticism in her voice.

"Why would she be pranking you? She's *your* aunt." I narrow my eyes at her. "I bet you're in on it. Is this one of your friends? Miss Butter-Churner?"

"Oh, definitely," she says, her voice dripping with sarcasm. "I just fucking love waking up at two a.m. to torment my aunt's hot neighbor after watching my entire life burn to the ground. This is my idea of fun." She waves her hand around, and the bag swings wildly enough that a trickle of herbs or whatever is in potpourri falls out.

Hot neighbor. She thinks I'm hot?

A low hum fills the air, and all the hair on my arms stands up.

"Ah, fucking hell." Tara steps closer to me, her hand brushing up against mine. "You feel that?"

"You expect me to believe you don't have something to do with this bullshit?"

"I think my aunt told me she had a ghost problem for a reason, and whatever this is... is the reason."

"Oh yeah. Sure, ghosts. That's what's been waking me up. Not the bucket list from hell in your hot pink rental from..." I pause, unable to think of the right word.

"From hell?" Tara suggests wryly. "If that's what's in hell—monster dildos and pink glitter—then I'll take a front-row seat."

"I'm going back to bed," I tell her. "Stay the hell off my property, and tell your singing friend to stay off it, too." I'm not yelling, not quite, but I definitely would like to.

"Tell her yourself. Little Miss Cottagecore is right there." Tara's voice is hushed, and her face goes pale at the sight of something behind me. "What do you want?"

"I want to *rest*."

I turn in time to see the current musical bane of my sleep schedule. Her old-timey dress hangs off her form in tatters, and her mouth gapes as she continues to scream the word rest.

"*Then go home and sleep!*" I bellow, sick of holding it in. "No one is making you bother us! For Christ's sake, just *go to sleep!*"

The woman blinks at me, and her mouth snaps shut.

It must be some special trick Tilly or Tara have rigged, but it looks like the woman just... vanishes.

"Oh fuck. I do not like this. Hell no. Nuh-uh. Nope." Tara, whose eyes are round and whose face is paper white, fervently shakes her head. "Fuck this. *Fuck.* I bet she lied about the mold and the pipes bursting just to make me deal with this. I don't believe in this garbage. I can't *believe* her."

"Good night," I snap at Tara. "And if you don't want me to pursue legal action, then you better tell your Aunt Tilly to stop fucking waking me up in the middle of the night."

"This wasn't Aunt Tilly." She shakes her head slowly. "That wasn't... that wasn't human."

"Nice try, but I'm not falling for any of your or your aunt's bullshit. I'm going to sleep, and I'm not selling my land. You two can go fuck yourselves. I know you have the supplies to do it." I roar the last bit, letting anger carry me.

"Rude," she says, fire erasing some of the fear in her face.

"Sorry," I say automatically. Why am I apologizing to her?

"Just calm down and listen to me; I swear I'm telling the truth. This isn't my aunt." Her face screws up, and the fog around us swirls, slowly dissipating.

"Why should I believe you? You saw that list the same as I did." I throw my hands up in the air. "I don't know why I'm even bothering to try to talk to you."

With that, I storm off, hopefully in the correct direction of my house and my bed.

Ghosts. She really wants me to believe we saw a ghost.

No fucking way am I falling for that.

5

Tara

I barely sleep the rest of the night. How the hell was I supposed to sleep after that?

I didn't think I believed in the supernatural, and yet here I am, frantically googling everything I can on... whatever Little Miss Haunted Cottagecore was. Is? Isn't?

She's not human. That's for damn sure. Maybe not super, but definitely... unnatural. I definitely do believe in things that are unnatural.

I cough, scrolling through another terrible-looking website about paranormal investigations and then nearly scream as a text vibrates through, startling me worse than the photo-shopped collage background, blue hyperlinks, and Comic Sans titling.

Emma: Are you okay?

Emma: text me back or else

Three dots appear, and I hastily tap out a message of my own before I find out exactly what "or else" means. I've had enough "or else" already today.

Me: I'm okay. Shop is not. I haven't even started dealing with insurance yet

Emma: Thank fuck you're okay. You'll figure the insurance stuff out. You're a bad bitch. Or should I say bad witch?

I laugh at her text, but honestly? It just makes me feel like shit. I lied to her all those months ago when we met. A year ago now, I sold her a book on spells so I could get out of the red for the day... and apparently my ghostly advice worked, because now Emma's convinced I'm the real deal.

Emma: I heard you're staying with your aunt?

Me: I am indeed at the Pussy Palace

Emma: I'm sorry, what?

Me: You have to see it to believe it—she turned the guest house into this... wild short-term vacation rental called the Pussy Palace

I snap a quick selfie of my shirt and send it as proof.

Me: Just be glad I took down the Great Wall Of Dildos

Emma: I have so many questions

Emma: I'm not really sure I should ask them

Emma: Listen, I know this might not be the best timing for you, and I don't want you to say yes if you're not ready or just not in the mood, but are you still up for holding down the fortune-telling booth at the hotel's fall festival? It's sold out

Emma: The festival and the hotel, believe it or not

I crow in delight, beyond thrilled for her.

Me: Fuck yeah it is! PR queen of New Hopewell. You've been pushing that haunted vibe, and this fall festival is going to be amazing

I scrunch my nose as I consider it. Do I want to go fake my way through a bunch of tarot readings for tourist and pretend I know what I'm doing?

I stare down at the airbrushed pink *Pussy Palace* lettering on the T-shirt, noticing the unicorn cat jumping through the letter *a*. Wow.

This shirt and the clothes I had on my back yesterday are all that's left of my life, and who knows how long it will be until insurance pays out.

Me: I will absolutely be there, with literal bells on

Me: Because I will be in full costume as your spooky tarot reading witch

Me: Meaning I'll be borrowing this weird scarf from my aunt that's trimmed in bells

Me: Since I have no clothes of my own to wear

Emma: Sounds like an awesome scarf—and I'm sorry about the clothes. I can't imagine how you're feeling right now

I sigh, thinking about my two-a.m. wake-up call. Song? Wake-up haunting?

I don't love this for me.

Me: Hey, do you still have that spell book you bought from me?

Guilt washes over me.

Me: I'll buy it back from you.

Emma: You can have it! I haven't had any issues in a few months

I swallow. As close as Em and I have become, I tune her out when she talks about her... ghost issues.

Bad friend alert.

Also, bad foresight yet again from a fake fortune teller.

Emma: I'd bring it to you, but I'm slammed. I'll see you at the vendor setup and info meeting tomorrow? Let me know if you need anything for your booth. I can help

Tomorrow? Shit. Is it October already? When did that happen?

Me: Nah, my aunt should have more than enough of that kind of thing. She won't mind helping with that. In fact, she'll love it

Emma: I'm so freaking glad you're still going to make it. The fall festival wouldn't be right without our town magic expert!!!

Me: I wouldn't miss it

I toss my phone across the couch and cover my face with my hands, groaning. God. I am not only an impostor of the highest order, but I am also a shitty friend.

Yawning, I stretch out. The watery morning light casts a pale beam across my skin. It doesn't feel like fall here. Not yet, anyway—it's much too hot and humid—but the sun does seem softer than its violent summer self.

I roll over on my side, and the events in the pine needle-covered forest bounce back through my head. Oh yeah, that's why I was scrolling like an over-caffeinated influencer—because I saw something.

I saw something in the woods with Ward Carlisle, and whatever it was scared the bejeezus straight out of my pores.

He saw it, too.

I know he did.

I stare out the windows. The pink velvet curtains glow where the sun hits them. A crow calls out, a harsh caw that makes me stiffen a little. Black feathers brush the window as it lands on the sill, and I sit bolt upright, shaking my head.

"Nope," I tell it. "I'm all set on this shit today. Hit my limit. Thanks, though."

Quick as I can, I cross over to the window and pull the curtains closed.

Very much not interested in a creepy crow. Would very much not recommend.

I thought I could go back to sleep? Ha!

I rake my fingers through my hair, and just like that, I decide it's time to walk to the main house and pump Tilly for some real answers.

Tilly knows something is going on, clearly.

"Shit." I plop back down on the couch. Going to Aunt Tilly means that I have to admit two things that I'd rather not admit.

One, that she was right. Tilly is insufferable about being right.

Two, I'll have to admit that I saw something in the woods.

That's by far the worst of the two options. Tilly will give me a knowing look and tell me for the millionth time that I have the gift, just like she does, but more powerful. Then I'll get the lecture about how I should use it, how I should open myself up to nature and the elements—blah, blah, blah—and how monetizing my gift is wrong.

I roll my eyes, grab a pillow, and loose a scream into it.

Frankly, it's surprising that Tilly didn't outright gloat that my whole life burned to a crisp. Color me mildly shocked that she didn't scream "I told you so!" and do a dance in front of the foamy fire retardant.

"Argh." I slam my fist on the arm of the couch, a choice I immediately regret.

Maybe I should snoop around the house some more. Figure out what Tilly's been up to by having a bunch of women up here, figure out what all the "complimentary" spell ingredients and recipes really make.

That is, if I can remember the shit Tilly taught me through my teenage years.

I used to know herb lore and her magic rituals like the back of my hand. Back when it all seemed fun and silly.

Now? I mostly use the herb lore to make custom loose-leaf teas and pretend to read them.

I locked down whatever part of me Tilly thought could "see" after it showed me things I didn't want to see. Things I couldn't forget.

Several different therapists have insisted that I was picking up on subconscious cues, that maybe what I remembered was different from reality.

All I know is I'm not ready to... do any of this.

But I also know I need sleep, and if this is some weird Tilly stunt, I want to find that out, too.

Of course, there is someone I can take my findings to and

ask for help. If it's not supernatural, which, of course, it's not, maybe we could get to the bottom of it together.

I clap my hands together.

I have a plan.

Snoop, gather evidence, and take my findings to my hot, angry, new partner in supernatural crime:

Ward Carlisle.

6

Ward

I slept. Not great, not a lot, but sleep did, in fact, happen.

Sure, it was plagued by nightmares of a girl churning butter with hair all over her face á la some early 2000s horror film. But dreams haunted by animal fats aside, I feel more like myself than I have in months.

Humming, I flip a pancake, grinning as it flops perfectly back into the pan. Bacon sizzles in the cast-iron pan next to it. Yeah, it's fucking lunchtime, and I slept through a Friday meeting I usually attend, but I cannot find one fuck to give.

All out of fucks.

Even the fact that I'm out of maple syrup doesn't bother me like it might have yesterday.

So when my doorbell rings, I'm smiling as I open it, bacon still cooking on the stove.

Tara.

She's still in her *Pussy Palace* shirt. She's bare-legged, with dirt speckling her calves and ankles, and she's got the ugliest shoes I've ever seen on her feet.

It shouldn't be so damn cute.

I stare at her for a second, trying to regain my bearings.

"We need to talk," she says, pushing past me. She cranes her neck as she looks around. "You do all this work yourself?"

A little pride shoots through me, and then I remember she's the enemy. At least, she's the niece of the enemy.

"What the hell are you doing here?" I ask.

"You weren't raised in Texas, were you?" she asks, her pretty lips quirked in amusement.

I glare at her, one hand on my hip as she floats past me into the kitchen, still staring around.

"If you were, you would have already offered me sweet tea or... coffee?" The word holds a note of hope, and if I wasn't so prejudiced against her, I might think it was cute.

"Why would I give you something to drink? I want you to leave."

Tara just laughs, though. In one hand, she's holding a bag of god only knows what. The other is tugging at the hem of her shirt. Her bare legs are summer tan, and the garment falls just long enough to cover her ass and just short enough to have me thinking about her ass.

A shirt that ugly shouldn't have me imagining her pussy palace, and yet, here I am, imagining it.

"Why are you still wearing that?"

"Did you not hear? News is all over town. My life burned to a crisp yesterday. In fact, I'm pretty sure my aunt told you that yesterday, right before you told us to fuck off." She tilts her head at me, fluttering long black eyelashes. "Well, the first time you told me to fuck off in the last twenty-four hours."

She steps closer. So close I can see flecks of gold in her dark brown eyes.

Damn.

"Or did you tell me to go fuck myself the second time?" Her voice is low and husky, and for a long moment, I'm speechless.

My brain is very active, though, thanks to getting some sleep, and it's imagining exactly what that would look like.

"Your bacon is burning, Ward Carlisle," Tara says, grinning at me.

"Fuck," I grunt.

She's right, and I only just manage to save the slices from a very hot death and give myself a nice grease burn in the process.

"You know, you could avoid a lot of burns if you wore a shirt. I assume your clothes didn't all burn up?" Tara's perched on one of my reclaimed wood barstools. The ugly shoes have been abandoned on the floor, and her bare feet are pointed on the top rung, her legs lovely in spite of the dirt.

I glance down at my bare chest, realizing with a start that I have, in fact, only ever been around Tara with my shirt off.

"No one's ever complained about that," I say, then try not to wince. No. Hell no. I am not flirting with her.

"Wasn't a complaint," she says slowly. "Just a comment, since you seemed offended by my clothes. Or is this a clothing-optional kind of place?"

A cheeky smile lights up her face, and I just stare at her, unsure what to say to that. She has to be joking.

She clears her throat. "Right. Well. I came over here because..." She trails off, and I methodically continue to make myself a plate of pancakes and bacon, then mentally curse at myself and make her one, too.

I set it in front of her with a grunt, along with a fork and knife, then settle onto a barstool at the end of the counter, putting plenty of space between us.

With her bare legs and my bare chest, we need more than a whole kitchen counter to stop me from thinking about bare skin, but I can't quite make myself sit at the table.

"How come I haven't ever seen you around town?"

"I don't like to go into town."

"You just live out here... by yourself? And you don't go into town?"

I can't blame her for the disbelief clear on her face.

"Aren't you lonely?"

"What I am is none of your business," I say, shoveling a bite of pancake into my mouth. The fucking audacity of this woman. Showing up half-naked on my doorstep, only to prattle on about my social habits or lack thereof.

"Fair enough. Thanks for the pancakes. You didn't have to give me any."

I half expect her to snark about eating them without syrup, but she cuts a tiny piece and chews politely, somehow managing to smile at me while she does so.

"You already shamed me about sweet tea once. I wasn't going to set myself up for more grief."

She laughs. It's an adorable sound. Her nose scrunches as she watches me watch her. "Smart. These are delicious, by the way. From scratch?"

"Pancake mix is a waste of money."

"Of course." The note of disbelief in her voice is drowned out by her sparkling smile, and I frown at her.

"Why are you here? What do you want, Tara?"

I immediately regret saying her name.

I won't be able to get the taste of it out of my mouth.

"I... Honestly, I don't know how to say this." Her hand trembles, and the fork clanks against the white plate. "It's about, uh, it's about last night."

I narrow my eyes.

"You came here to apologize?"

"Huh?" She gapes at me.

I take a bite of bacon, then set it down carefully on the plate. Coffee. I need coffee.

"Why would I apologize?" Her voice has an edge to it, sharp enough to cut. "I didn't have anything to do with that."

"So you're apologizing on behalf of your aunt."

I pull out two cups and pour steaming coffee into both, then set one in front of her before returning to my spot, my safe distance from her.

"No. God. No. Just let me... let me have a second." She stares at the coffee, makes a face, and hops out of her chair, her shirt catching on the stool.

My brain short-circuits.

Tara isn't wearing underwear.

I chug the coffee, like I can physically burn the image of her round ass out of my brain by scalding my throat.

Not my brightest of moments.

She opens up the fridge, somehow unaware or uncaring of the fact that I now have a massive hard-on thanks to the covert view of her left ass cheek. Without another word, she pulls out the carton of milk and gives it an experimental sniff before shrugging and adding some to her cup.

"Want some milk?" I ask, trying for snark and managing to sound hoarse instead. I clear my throat.

"Little late, but yes, thank you. Sugar?"

"In the container by the fridge."

"This is cute," she says, smiling at the dainty white and blue sugar bowl. A tiny mouse acts as the handle of the lid, and her teeth flash as she uses the matching tongs to pull a cube out and set it in her coffee. "You have this, and you drink yours black?"

My throat gets tight. "None of your fucking business."

"Right, then. Okay. Right. So, what is my business, then, is whatever the hell happened last night."

"Your aunt's schemes."

"No, I don't think so."

She shoves the bag I'd nearly forgotten across the counter to me, then sits down again. I mentally pat myself on the back for not trying to catch another flash of ass. I don't need blue balls to match the hard-on that doesn't seem to want to go away.

"My aunt... she believes in... er, magic." Pink colors her cheeks.

Inside the bag are dozens of little potpourri bags. "And perfume?" I cough, because damn, that lavender smell is strong.

"Those are protection sachets," she says quietly. "I know... if you've heard of me, you might know." She tilts her head back, making a guttural sound of frustration.

I hardly hear it. I'm too entranced by the smooth expanse of her neck, wondering if she smells like lavender, too.

"Okay, Tara, just fucking say it." Her cheeks are glowing pink as she turns fully to me, her jaw twitching. "I make a living—made a living—pretending to... do the magic my Aunt Tilly taught me. I know it probably sounds so, so stupid, but Tarot, Kolache and Tea? That was my store. It burned down." She pinches the bridge of her nose, her eyes watering.

No, not watering. She's about to cry.

Either she's a damn good actress or she means whatever it is she's trying to say.

"I faked it. Mostly. Tarot is easy enough. The cards mean things. You tell the person what they mean, and they draw inferences about their own lives from it."

"What does this have to do with last night?" I ask gruffly, although I think I know where she's headed.

I don't like it.

Goose bumps stand out on my arms, and she turns paler.

"I never thought I really... I never thought it was real, you know? But I know what I saw last night, and I know what Tilly's been having all those women who stay at that house do."

"Torment me." I snort.

"Look in the bag." She's deadly serious for the first time since I've seen her, and it's making me slightly uncomfortable.

I pull out a pink pad of paper. "Pink."

"Read it." Her voice is a whisper.

I do, scanning it. "It's a recipe." I squint at the bottom paragraph. It doesn't call for baking or mixing or whatever else I expected.

Nope. It calls for singing. At midnight.

"It's a protection spell. She put all her renters to magical work and sold it to them as women's empowerment. I think... I don't think what we saw last night is a prank."

My jaw twitches, and I raise my eyebrow. "How convenient."

"What? No. I think... I think there might really be a ghost." Her eyes are huge. "I think there's a reason we were both there last night. I think... I think we should try and fix this... together."

Together. Just like that, my carnal interest in Tara fades away. Not because of her cuckoo hypothesis, but because of the idea that I need to be together. With her.

I don't do together, not anymore.

My stomach turns, and I push the plate of pancakes away.

"Get out of my house."

"Wait, what?"

"I'm not working with you on this. I don't know you. I don't trust you. Why should I believe anything you're saying?"

"Because you were there. *You saw it*. I know you saw it. You saw it, right?" Her voice is frantic, and her eyes wild. They dart between mine, like she can't quite figure out my reaction.

"I saw whatever it was your aunt wanted me to see." I wipe my mouth on a napkin. "Tell your dear old aunt that I'm not fucking moving, so she can quit sending in frauds do her dirty work."

Tara's jaw drops, and shock colors her face. "Did you just call me a fraud?"

"You called yourself one," I say, but the insult doesn't bring me the satisfaction it should.

She marches over to me and tears the pink spell pad out of my hands, one watery tear streaking down her cheek. The bag crinkles as she shoves it back inside.

"Thank you ever so much for brunch." Carefully, she drains her coffee cup before slamming it back onto the counter. "And now it's my turn to tell you to go fuck yourself."

I deserved that.

She tosses one of the purple potpourri bags at me, and I catch it reflexively. "If you're not an idiot, you'll put that under your pillow tonight. Or maybe you do deserve sleep deprivation."

With that, Tara whirls around and storms out of the kitchen... only to return, still scowling at me.

"I'll be liberating these," she says, waving her two remaining pancakes at me. "Good luck with the ghost, asshole."

I can't help but check out her legs again as she walks away.

And if I tuck the potpourri bag under my pillow that night? It's out of desperation for sleep.

7

Tara

I t's October second, but Texas hasn't gotten the memo that it's supposed to be fall. The vermilion velvet cloth over my sad little booth manages to keep the sun off me, but it also seems to trap the humidity.

I'm sticky all over and hoping that the lack of people is because the festival's only just kicked off and not a sign of what's to come for the rest of the month.

"Hey," Em says, holding two iced drinks in sweating plastic cups. "Love your ensemble. Very witchy. Very now." She stares at me and my booth in clear awe.

I clear my throat, feeling more uncomfortable than ever, then push the sheer fabric Tilly draped like a hood on me farther off my head. It tinkles musically, because it does, in fact, have bells.

"It's too much," I say, awkward and uncomfortable. It's a costume in more ways than one. Fake clothes for the big fraud.

"Not at all. It's perfect. You look gorgeous. Love the makeup."

Tilly insisted on dolling me up for today. I obliged, simply because seeing her happy made me happy, too. Besides, I haven't replaced any makeup of my own. I cast a long look at the pretty crystal vase hung with a sign that says *tips*.

It's not pussy palace neon pink, but hopefully it will still work.

That or the deep plum lipstick and sparkling smoky eyes will make everyone take pity on me.

"Thanks," I manage belatedly. "It feels weird to have so much on."

"Well, you look great. Here." She plops one of the plastic cups onto the table. The ice cubes tinkle against each other as they melt. "It's slow, isn't it?"

"It's the first day," I tell her. "We've only been open for a minute. I bet as soon as the sun sets, people will come out."

She sips from her orange- and white-striped paper straw, unconvinced, as she scans the few couples.

"It looks so great, Em. Seriously. The hotel is stunning. I still can't believe how amazing the restoration turned out. Plus all this?" I wave a hand around, my many costume rings (also Tilly's) catching the fading sunlight. Several dozen booths like mine make a maze throughout the cleared acreage, all with different colored velvet sun-sails. It smells like cider donuts and coffee and vanilla pumpkin bread. "It's like a movie set. Please. People are going to be coming in from miles away to see this. It's fantastic."

It really is, too. The vibe is adorable and pretty and autumnal. All the decorations are tasteful and vintage-inspired, from black cat and moon banners, to oversized potted mums and sunflowers, to lime green sweet potato vines trailing over hay bales. Pumpkins are everywhere, as are strands of garland strung with glittering leaves in every shade of red and orange.

It's stunning, and while I look around, a gaggle of small

children lines up to take photos with their faces stuck through a few stand-up wooden characters. They're precious.

"Look," I tell her, pointing. "Those pictures are going to go up on social media, and every parent is going to want that same photo. You're going to be a total hit."

"Is that what your tarot cards told you?" she asks. There's a hint of desperation in her question that makes me slightly queasy.

"Do you want me to do a reading for you?" I bat my eyelashes, resting my chin on my hands. "I could use the practice. I feel rusty."

What I feel, actually, is fucking nervous. I've been on edge since the sleepless night when I saw Madame Butter-Ghost, and even though I haven't seen or heard or... sensed anything else, I can't shake the feeling that whatever the hell was happening, it's not over yet.

Doesn't help that Ward completely spit in my face when I tried to confide in him about it. I mean, on one hand, I don't blame him. I came over to his house half out of my mind from fear and lack of sleep, and also only half-dressed.

"Are you okay?" Em asks, peering into my face.

"Huh?"

"I asked you a question and you just... zoned out."

"Sorry. I'm sorry."

"No, it's no big deal. I was just asking if you liked iced pumpkin lattes." She frowns at my untouched drink.

"It's fall. It's a crime not to have a pumpkin latte, and iced sounds perfect." I take the cup, the condensation slicking my palms, and take a sip. It's full of cinnamon, and the espresso is strong. And the pumpkin flavor does, in fact, taste like autumn.

A slow smile curls my lips, and I relax a little, exhaling some of the tension that's knotted my shoulders for days now.

"Good?"

"So good. Thank you, Em."

"Did the book help?"

The spell book. I wince, because she took the time to bring it to me at the meeting for vendors, and I've hardly had a chance to open it.

That, and I really don't want to. I don't want to do anything that might a cause ghee-ghost reappearance.

"Hi there, are you open?" A pretty blond woman blinks at me wearing a smile that I immediately peg as fake. I know her type immediately. Anyone who works in the kind of field I do would, too.

She doesn't really want a reading.

She wants to prove how wrong I am.

At times like this, with customers like her, I'm not mad about my own petty, stubborn streak.

"Of course," I say, dropping my voice half an octave. "Sit down and hear your future."

The man behind her snorts, elbowing her in the hip.

Em shoots me an amused smile, backing up a respectful distance to let me work.

I lean forward and stare at the couple, who exchange grins I can only describe as bitchy.

"Would you like a—"

"Tarot," she says succinctly. "Not that it matters."

"Are you sure?" I say, fluttering my lashes at her and pretending like I'm not insulted. I mean, I mostly make this stuff up, but she doesn't have to be downright rude. It's disrespectful. I point to the chalkboard where Tilly painstakingly hand-lettered a price list. "I can do palms, crystal ball work, and, although that's less precise, tea leaves." I gesture to the tins of pretty loose-leaf teas I made myself, alongside stacks of pumpkin orange- and cream-striped paper cups. An electric kettle's plugged into a power strip I've hidden underneath a dark purple tablecloth.

"I also sell the tea by the quarter pound in resealable, compostable bags," I add in a businesslike voice.

"How convenient," she simpers, and the man with her snickers an ugly laugh.

"Isn't it?" I smile at her slowly, the kind of evil smile that I use to show that I know exactly the kind of person she is.

Pretty on the outside and jack-o'-lantern rotten on the inside.

"Are you going to read the cards, or what?" She holds up her hands, inspecting her French manicure.

"Pick a deck," I tell her, setting three in front of me to choose from. Tilly had no shortage of tarot decks. In fact, she's borderline hoarding them. She gave me *fifteen* to bring here, telling me what she's told me for years—that I have to find a deck I connect with, but in the meantime, let the customers help me pick which one they want. I hardly glanced at the decks she loaded into a box for me, but the few I saw were gorgeous. One watercolored and illustrated, another gold-foiled art deco style.

I almost can't judge Tilly for hoarding them. They're works of art.

The woman doesn't take her eyes off me. She doesn't even glance at the cards.

"The middle one." She points, examining her fingernails again, and I realize she's not actually looking at her nails, but at the massive diamond on her ring finger. "It doesn't matter."

I sniff. Disrespectful.

"The cards call to us," I say, slipping into a version of the monologue Tilly so loves to give me. "Each deck has a different personality. You've chosen the..."

I pause, because I haven't seen a deck like this in a long time.

"Dragging this out won't earn you a bigger tip," she says.

"This is a Thoth deck," I say, ignoring her. I shuffle the deck with practiced ease, my fingers tingling on contact with the cards. "Most tarot decks are Rider-Waite. You know, the yellow-backed ones? Classic. This is not used as often, but it is a beautiful deck."

The lady makes a noise of slight disagreement, and I try not to glare at her.

I spread the cards out in front of me, staring at the glittering black and gold backs of the cards. "Aleister Crowley designed this type of deck in the 1930s."

The woman's fiancé coughs, and it sounds suspiciously like "fake history."

What a charmer. He might even give Ward a run for his rude money.

Ward's a hell of a lot cuter, though.

"I'm going to do a three-card spread," I say out loud, mostly for myself, because it's been a while since I worked with this type of deck. Better to keep it simple. Sometimes the typical Celtic cross layout doesn't work quite right for these cards.

The woman yawns, her diamond blinding as she covers her mouth with her hand.

I hand the deck to her. "Cut it."

She does so with a simpering smile that makes me want to kick her in the shins. I don't, though, because my foot has better places to be.

I take the deck back from her, and I don't need a psychic to tell me this woman is full of bad energy.

I lay the three cards out, turning them over slowly. She's watching carefully now. Whether with curiosity or in hopes of waiting for me to slip up or something, I don't know.

A tingle of awareness I haven't felt in years sluices down my spine, and I stiffen.

"Lust," I say in a low voice, running my finger down the

illustration. A naked woman writhing on the back of a human-lion hybrid. "This card could mean several things."

"Typical," the lady sighs. "Is this something I could find out via google?"

I've had about enough of her shit. I stare at her, tugging the sheer hood back up to my forehead. "The cards are just cards. How you choose to interpret their meaning is the important part. You will know what they mean to you."

She sighs, rolling her eyes, and I bite back a really shitty response that would definitely not help me make money at the festival this month.

Might be worth it, though. It could be part of my schtick.

Fortune telling with a side of bitchiness could be my new motto.

"Are you going to finish?" she says, twirling her finger at me.

"Lust, in this position, likely means aggression of some form in your life. Disappointment in your lot. Maybe in how things have ended up." I smile sweetly at her.

She glares at me.

Right.

"Five of discs," I say in a sing-song voice.

"I've heard enough of this bullshit. Come on, Becca. Let's go." The man behind her twirls a wedding ring on his finger, eyeing the beer garden at the end of the maze of vendors.

"Five of discs could signify change. Failure, crisis..." I trail off, because it's not a great card.

"I've heard enough," the woman says crisply.

"That will be twenty dollars," I tell her. I point to a laminated QR code. "Venmo is fine. Cash is, too. However you would like to pay."

"You didn't finish the reading. Why should I pay?"

The last card is an upright hanged man. I swallow. Maybe it's better I don't finish it, after all.

"Fair enough. It's on me, then. Enjoy your honeymoon."

She starts at that, and I take petty satisfaction in the fact that I've surprised her. I watch the unhappy couple drift over to the beer garden, and I wonder how long their marriage will last. Unhappy people tend not to make each other happy.

I may not be a relationship expert, but I do know that.

I sigh, shuffling the cards on autopilot, then put them back into a neat stack on the table and sip my drink.

"Well, look at you," a familiar voice says, and when I nearly jump out of my skin.

Ward Carlisle stands in front of me, dressed in a snug T-shirt and jeans, looking more at home among the magical autumn décor than he has anywhere else. Mouthwatering.

"What's that?" he asks, squinting at me.

My cheeks heat. Dear god, did I say that out loud? "Thirsty." I hold up a finger to him and suck at the iced pumpkin spice latte like my dignity is somewhere at the bottom of it.

"Did you want your fortune told?" I ask him, not sure what I want him to say.

He scoffs.

Well, I guess I didn't want him to do that.

"Beer garden is over there," I say, pointing to it and wearing a smile as fake as the one the awful woman who was just sitting in the chair in front of me wore. "Though I don't expect you to stay long enough to finish a whole beer, considering how anti-social you are."

I expect a mean retort, or a fuck off, or something.

What I don't expect is for Ward Carlisle to turn white as a ghost as he stares at the blond woman with a glass stein in her hand.

The same blond woman who was just sitting in front of me.

She kisses her fiancé while Ward watches. I, on the other hand, look from her to Ward and back again. He runs a hand through his dark hair, rumpling it adorably, with a look of shock and despair on his face.

"What's wrong?" I ask him. "Are you okay?" I lean forward on my elbows. "Is it the butter churning phantom?"

Then he says four little words that change everything.

"I need your help."

8

Ward

Tara's expression shifts from worried and curious to a devilish grin. Her dark-painted lips are a shade that makes me think of biting into a plum.

My heart's hammering against my chest so fast that my stomach flips, and I sink into the folding chair in front of her booth, my breath hard to catch.

"I am, in fact, open for business." She folds her hands, laden with heavy rings, in front of her. Bracelets jingle on her wrists when she moves her hands, and I can't stop staring at her. This is not the woman who was half-dressed in my kitchen two days ago, telling me that ghosts are real and running a long con on behalf of her aunt.

Her eyes are lined in dark, glittering makeup. Sheer fabric mostly hides the brown waves that fall across her shoulders.

For a moment, I'm so transfixed by her that I forget what it is, exactly, we're talking about.

Then I hear it: my ex-girlfriend's high-pitched laugh, and my ears start ringing.

"I need your help. Right now."

"Oh my god."

I hear her call out, and I know I've been spotted. What the fuck is she doing here? I moved here partly to get away from her, to get away from the fact that she left me for him, managed to turn our mutual friends against me, and spread an absolute shit-ton of rumors about me. And now she's here?

"Is that Ward Carlisle?"

I wince.

"Oh..." Tara's eyes go round, and her jaw drops open. "She's coming back over here."

"I need your help," I say desperately, looking around wildly.

"I don't think my shawl is big enough to hide you," she says, biting her cheeks and clearly trying not to laugh.

"I need you to play along." It comes out thick with stress. "I need you to help me. Can you play along?"

"Why should I?" she asks, folding her arms.

My stomach knots.

"Ward! I know that's you. Oh my god, honeybun, look who it is," Becca calls.

"What do you want?" I ask, sweat beading along my fore-head, and a tension headache starting to pulse behind my eyes. "What do you want for playing along?"

"That depends," she says. "That horrible woman is coming over here with her disgusting husband."

"Husband?" I grit my teeth. Fuck. I do not want to see them. I do not want to play nice. "They're married?"

Of fucking course she married him. My blood pressure rises.

"Yeah, and if the cards are right—"

"*Ward!*" Becca calls again, and when I glance away from Tara, my ex is headed toward us like a heat-seeking missile. Fuck.

"I'll give your aunt the land she wants. I'll have a lawyer and the county redraw our property lines. I'll do whatever it takes. Help you hunt the ghost or whatever. I don't care. Just play along. I'm begging you."

Her eyebrows rocket up to her hairline, disbelief clear on her lovely face.

"What do you want me to do?" she asks.

"Pretend to be mine." It comes out on a growl.

I should have said "my girlfriend" or "my fiancée" or anything else, but once I say it, I know it's what I need... for Becca to believe that Tara is mine. That we belong together.

"Pretend that we're in love," I add.

"Oh my goodness, Ward. What are you doing here? Devon, can you believe it? You remember Ward, right?"

I tilt my head, memorizing Tara's expression as it flits between disbelief and then a coy cunning that makes my heart stand still.

She finally nods, and I turn and stand, holding out a hand to Devon.

"Hey, Becca. Devon," I say, unable to keep the ice out of my voice. He shakes my hand too firmly, the set of his mouth clearly saying he's as unhappy as I am that Becca's dragged him over here. He squeezes it again, like he's got something to prove.

"I hear congratulations are in order."

Becca squeals, and I wonder how I ever found the sound anything but obnoxious. "Thank you," she gushes, simpering as she holds her hand up for me to inspect. "Isn't it gorgeous? Oh, is this so hard for you?" she pouts, blinking slowly like she's just realized this might not be fun for me.

I can't believe I never saw how vicious she could be until she turned it on me.

"Oh, Devon, we're making Ward uncomfortable. We should have stayed in the beer tent." Becca puts her arm around Devon's waist, and I just stare, unable to think past all the hurt that aches like a phantom limb. "We shouldn't rub our happy ending in his face."

"Why not?" Tara pipes up. Pushing her hood all the way off her head, she stands and joins me on the other side of the table. Her small hand reaches up, squeezing my shoulder, and I blink, remembering what I just promised her. "Ward has never said anything but lovely things about both of you. You must be his ex, right?"

Tara beams at Becca. "I can't believe you ever let this little schnookums go," she continues, and I let out a surprised grunt as she pinches the hell out of my ass. "This body and this face? I owe you a thank-you card. Heck, maybe a whole thank-you dinner." Tara sighs happily, turning a besotted smile on me.

"You two are... together?" Becca asks, giving Tara a pointed up-and-down look.

"Oh yeah," Tara says, smacking my ass. I jump a little. "Best sex of my life. Holy cow." She whistles, then fans her face. "I didn't think I was going to survive that many orgasms, but that thing he does with his tongue—"

"We've been dating for two years now," I interrupt, tugging Tara into my side and squeezing her hard, trying to shut her the hell up.

"Still feels brand new, doesn't it, baby?" Tara bats her eyelashes up at me.

Maybe this wasn't the best idea.

"Brand new," I agree.

She slaps my ass again, hard, and I turn my curse into a cough.

"Brand spanking new," she adds, laughing.

"Aren't you two... so *cute*." Becca looks like she bit into a sour lemon.

Worth it.

"Oh, disgustingly cute," Tara says, managing another ass pinch.

"Honey, you keep squeezing that, and we're going to have a problem on our hands," I grit out.

"Then I better keep doing it," she says in a stage whisper, winking outrageously at Becca.

"We're on the first leg of our honeymoon here," Becca interjects, rubbing a hand up and down Devon's chest. "We're having a great time, aren't we? This little town in Hickville, who knew Podunk could be so cute?" She sighs.

"So adorable," Tara agrees. I bat her hand away from my chest before her pinching fingers find my nipple. "It was *so* easy to fall in love here, wasn't it, Ward?" She looks up at me with huge doe eyes, and I blink at her in disbelief.

She's laying it on so thick I almost buy the crap she's selling. And I'm the one who put her up to it.

"It is, it is," Becca says emphatically. "I just want to kiss Devon all the time—"

"You do?" Devon's forehead wrinkles in confusion.

"Yes, honey. Of course." Becca giggles. "Kiss me now. I just can't keep my hands off you," she insists.

My stomach turns as Devon tilts his face down, and it's like watching a train wreck.

Tara plants her hands on my cheeks and forces me to look at her.

She raises her eyebrows, and I know what she's asking.

When she rises up onto her tiptoes, I don't hesitate.

And when our lips meet, I forget how to breathe.

9

Tara

Three things flash through my mind.

I'm kissing Ward Carlisle.

I'm making out with him in public.

Oh my god, he's a *great* kisser.

Delight and desire course through me, as unexpected as his mouth on mine, as his hands gentle at my waist.

"Is this a kissing booth?" a red-haired teenager asks hopefully, and I break off the kiss.

Ward's staring down at me with a dark, unreadable expression, and Becca's staring at me with pure hatred.

Wonderful.

"Nope, but I can tell your fortune for a fee," I say.

"Yeah, she's a fortune teller," Becca sneers.

"Will my fortune show I get to kiss you?" the kid asks.

Ward finally stops staring at me, swiveling his attention to the gangly teenager.

"No one is kissing her but me," he growls.

Becca lets out an awkward laugh.

"Come sit down," I tell the kid, trying to push down the warmth that bubbles up at Ward's possessive phrase. He's just pretending.

I know all about that.

"We're here for the next two weeks," Becca tells him.

"Can you read my palm?" the teenager asks, a starry-eyed expression on his face.

"Sure," I say. "Palm readings are twenty. Hand on the table."

"A woman who knows her worth." The kid nods. "I like it."

I bite back a laugh, and when I glance up at Ward, he's wearing a thunderous expression that doesn't look fake at all. Not one bit.

"So, will you two meet us for dinner this weekend?" Becca asks.

Devon scowls, clearly none too pleased at Becca inviting her ex to dinner on their honeymoon.

I raise my eyebrows as I stare at the teen's palm.

"Does it say I'm going to kiss the fortune teller from the fair?"

"Not this fortune teller, nope," I say, and this time, I don't bother holding in my laugh. "Sorry, dude. I'm taken, and you're pissing off my boyfriend." I jerk my chin at Ward, who is completely ignoring Becca, who seems very put off by it.

"He doesn't treat you as well as I would."

"Kid." I shake my head, laughing. "I'm probably twice your age."

"I have a thing for cougars."

I touch his palm, and he sighs.

That's enough of that.

"All right, your palm says that if you keep hitting on me, you might get physically hurt by my boyfriend. It also says that you should listen to women when they tell you no, or your love life is going to suffer. Oh," I squint at the callouses on his hands. "And keep practicing... guitar?"

"Bass," he says, wide-eyed. "How did you know?"

"Ah-ah," I say, shaking a finger at him. "I can't give away my secrets."

"Cool. Very cool." He scans the QR code, and my phone buzzes as his payment hits my account.

"Have fun," I tell him.

"Make good choices," Ward says, threat implicit in his tone.

I cross my arms over my chest.

"So, dinner? Or? I'd love to tell everyone back home that we had a chance to see each other. Oh, or, you know what? Devon, oh my god, you know that little hole in the wall brewery? The same one that has that... tent here? They should come do that fall cider tasting with us next week. It's in a couple of days. Is that too soon? I know you hate taking time off work to be with people." Her sugary tone turns decidedly nasty. "It starts at eleven. They have a lunch to go with it."

Ward finally turns to face Becca. "We'll be there. Wouldn't miss it."

"Absolutely," I agree. "Love a good cider tasting. The Salt Circle is amazing. You know they were featured in *Food & Wine* magazine last month? They're not exactly a hole in the wall."

"That's so cute," she sneers at me, and my hand begins to raise of its own accord. Ward grabs my wrist, then kisses dramatically up my arm.

Becca grinds her teeth.

"*Great.* Good." She claps her hands. "Your mother will be thrilled to hear we've been in touch."

A muscle twitches in Ward's jaw. "You still talk to my mom?"

"Of course. We're in the same Junior League chapter. Remember, silly?" Becca gives a girly little giggle, and my lip curls.

"He's just such a silly goose," I say. "The first time he came out to my manor, I remember thinking, wow, what a silly goose."

Becca blinks at me, and to be honest, I'm not really sure what I'm talking about either. I'm pretty sure his lips on my skin short-circuited any remaining brain cells.

"Oh yeah," I continue, apparently not able to shut the fuck up. "He came out to the old family estate. My aunt has this stunning, I mean, absolutely stunning collection of monster—"

Ward shoves the straw to my iced pumpkin spice latte in my mouth, and I give him the evil eye as I sip it.

"Of monster-themed pottery," I finally finish. "Vintage. Eclectic. Heirloom quality."

Ward exhales in relief.

"How... charming," Becca says, staring at me like I've grown a second head.

"Isn't it, though? Well, you know what it's like to have too much money and time, right?" I'm talking out of my ass, because I certainly don't know either of those things, but it's clear Becca would like to think she does.

"Hmph. Devon, let's go try that sour cherry beer."

"The Salt Circle's sour cherry is my favorite," I tell her cheerfully. "See you at the Salt Circle's cider tasting in a few days!" I keep waving like a fool as they walk off, Becca with a pissy expression, and Devon looking like he'd rather chew his arm off than spend another minute with me. Big mood, buddy, big mood.

I take another swig of my pumpkin spice latte and grin up at Ward.

"My aunt's going to want to have you over for dinner so you two can go over all the details together," I tell him.

Maybe it makes me a shitty person to revel in his discomfort... and Becca's, too, but I can't say I'm not enjoying this.

"Don't make me regret this," he says in a low voice. "We have a deal until Halloween? Until they leave?"

"Oh, I will absolutely make you regret it. I most definitely will." I tap one finger against my cheek. "And yeah, I can fake it until Halloween. Or did you forget that you were talking to a total fraud?" I waggle my eyebrows, resentment at that comment still burning deep inside me.

"Takes one to know one" is all he says, though, walking away.

I watch him walk until someone asks about having their cards read. My phone buzzes with a Venmo alert, and I glance at it.

Ward: $5 for kissing booth

Another alert dings in.

Ward: $5 to text me when you get done

His phone number's there, too, and a small, self-satisfied smile plays across my lips as a small line begins to form at my booth.

Then I'm too busy shuffling cards and reading people to think too hard about Ward Carlisle.

But that doesn't mean I don't think about him... in fact, my mouth still seems to be tingling from that kiss.

10

Ward

Becca's right about one thing: I do hate having to take time off work. Even working remotely, I like my routine. I like my schedule, I like the predictability, and I like being at home. Grumbling, I pull on a soft flannel button-down and rake a hand through my hair, calling it good enough.

Fucking Becca.

I loved her so much, but it seems like a lifetime ago.

She was everything I thought I wanted: she was a member of the right country club, in my mom's social circle and thus coming with a stamp of parental approval, and she fit the image of the life I thought I wanted.

Nothing I did was ever good enough for her, though.

I stare at my reflection in the mirror, and I wonder how long I let that guide my own feelings of good enough.

I wonder how much of what she disliked about me in the end was real.

I'm not an easy man to live with.

That's why I live by myself now, away from people, away from the people who were only too ready to believe her sob story about how I never paid attention to her, how her coworker was there for her when I wouldn't bother...

There might have been some truth to that.

She put our entire relationship on display for all of our friends. Becca made our break-up into performance art, and when she was done with me, they weren't our friends anymore. They were hers.

"Fuck," I groan, pinching the bridge of my nose. "Why?"

Why did I agree to this? I told myself I didn't give a shit what those people thought, what Becca thought, about any of it.

And here I am, dancing to her tune all over again.

A text buzzes through my phone, and I pick it up like it's a venomous snake, like my ruminations have summoned Becca's texts all over again.

It's from an unknown number, and relief washes over me. My shoulders loosen, my breath comes easier, and I think I might even be smiling as I read the message.

Unknown: Uh, so, I hate to bug you, but my aunt can't bring me to the brewery today and I don't have a car

Unknown: I never needed one when I lived in town

Unknown: This is Tara, btw

Me: I can pick you up

Tara: Thank you so much

Me: yeah, of course. I should have offered. Us arriving together will only help sell it, you know?

Tara: Oh, good point. I didn't even think of that

Me: You're not going to talk about monster dildos today, right?

Shit. I don't know why I brought that up. I shouldn't have brought that up.

Tara: I'm fucking dying laughing. I don't know why I started to talk about that. Good god, I panicked

I let out a laugh of my own. The whole situation is so absurd that some more of the tension in my chest eases with the laughter.

Tara: Although, if you remember, it was her vintage monster pottery collection

Me: Heirloom quality

Tara: Should we come up with a cover story? Like, the how we met details? Work it all out?

Shit. I pull on my boots, thinking fast. A steady patter of rain pings against the windows. Looks like the cold front the meteorologists said would be here a few days ago has finally arrived.

Tara: I have an idea

I raise an eyebrow at the phone, like she'll be able to see my skepticism.

Tara: We were at the same shop, and we reached for the same set of butt plugs at the same time. It was love at first anal encounter

I bark out a startled laugh, swiping a hand down my face. This woman is... something else.

Tara: That was a joke. I would never bring up butt plugs on a first date

Me: You just did

Tara: This isn't a date, this is pre-game texting. This is the warm-up

Me: I must not know the dating etiquette when it comes to sex toys

Me: I can't say I've ever texted about butt plugs

Tara: Me neither, but that's why we're in love, you know? You filled the hole in my...

Me: Jesus

Tara: Heart

My own laugh startles me, and I grab an umbrella and my raincoat.

Tara: I'm at the main house—I had to borrow some clothes from my aunt.

Me: I'll be there in ten

Tara: Seriously, I promise to be on my best behavior

I should be relieved by that text.

But part of me wants to see just how outrageous this woman can be.

11

Tara

Aunt Tilly's closet always enchanted me, and even as a thirty-year-old woman, I'm still amazed. She converted one of the small first-floor rooms into a huge walk-in closet, and custom cabinetry houses all sorts of treasures accumulated over the course of her life.

What can I wear today that will be just right to play the part of his girlfriend?

I run my hands over a drawer full of vintage concert T-shirts.

What can I wear today that will make Ward smile?

That thought stops my hands in their tracks, and I blink, surprised at myself. When did I start wanting to make him smile?

Probably because it's a challenge. I've always loved a challenge. Always loved when someone told me I couldn't do something. Fuel for the petty fires.

Shit. I don't have time to think too hard about this. I need to pick something out to wear, and I need to do it now. Or, ya know, five minutes ago. Or thirty.

"Focus, Tara!" I yell at myself, in pure drill-sergeant mode.

Okay, Becca said Junior League, which means preppy, pretty, polished.

I take out one of Tilly's sweater dresses, twisting my mouth to the side as I consider it.

"That's my favorite funeral dress."

"Hey," I say over my shoulder. "I don't know what to wear. I have... five minutes."

"Your birthday suit."

"Mmm, I think that might be too formal for a cider tasting."

"Good call, good call. Don't want to make everyone feel underdressed."

I grin at Tilly.

"Why would you pick out that dress? That's not like you at all."

"I don't know," I confess. "I... wanted to look right. I guess. Proper?"

Tilly's lip curls in disgust. "There's a time and place for proper, but a brewery is not one of them. Wear something fun. Oh, you know what, hon? I have the cutest dress—I bought it a few years ago and never actually wore it, but it would be perfect on you."

Hangers squeak on the rod as she rummages through garments, and then her wrinkled face lights up as she pulls out a burgundy corduroy dress.

"Oh," I breathe, falling in love instantly. It's super weird and whimsical and adorable. Little orange pumpkins with green vines are embroidered all over it, and the straps are the kind you'd see on overalls.

"You love it?" She holds it against her body, swaying from side to side.

"I do. I really do."

"Here, it's chilly out today." She holds the dress up to me, and I take it as she pulls out a creamy balloon-sleeved sweater. "Wear this under it and..." Her voice grows muffled as she crouches down beneath a rack of pants. Then she emerges with a pair of black Mary-Jane Doc Martens.

"Oh my god," I breathe, staring at them. They're in mint condition and totally adorable.

"I wore these once, about two decades ago. They were a little big on me, but you're a smidge taller... will they fit?"

I take them reverently. "They're an eight? Yeah, that's my size."

"You can have them."

"Aunt Tilly!"

"Don't Aunt Tilly me," she says. "They don't fit. You're doing me a favor. You know, maybe you can help me get this under control. You need clothes, and I have more than I need. You can shop in Tilly's closet."

I set the shoes down carefully and wrap her in an embrace. "Thank you. I'm so lucky to have you in my life."

"Oh, don't get all sappy on me." She pulls away, beaming despite her words, and then waves a hand at me. "You better get dressed if you don't want to wear your birthday suit."

I do, tossing on the sweater and dress, grateful I could at least wash my underwear in Tilly's guest house. The sweater is a soft cashmere dream, about one hundred times nicer than anything I've ever owned, and the corduroy overall dress? God, it's so freaking cute, and even though it's a little tight in the waist, I have a feeling it will stretch out.

The Docs?

Fucking perfection.

I'm smiling as I step out of her closet, and Tilly claps her hands in delight.

"You're a vision in pumpkins."

"Excellent. That's exactly the vibe I was going for."

A door slams upstairs, and we both glance up.

"The house makes noise." The words stumble over each other in her hurry to say them. "You know how old houses are. Been worse since the... ah, pipes burst."

"You're so lucky it didn't ruin your closet," I tell her, shaking my head. "I love this outfit." I do a twirl for her.

"It looks like it was made for you. Now, tell me, who are you trying to impress?" She skewers me with a knowing look, and my eyes go wide.

"Just... you know. Everybody." It's a lie, and I don't realize it until it's left my mouth.

For whatever stupid reason, I want to impress one person in particular.

We both swivel to the front window as an SUV pulls up, and my heart skips a beat as Ward gets out of the driver's seat, looking absolutely delicious in a green and navy plaid flannel. He's rolled the sleeves up, showing up tanned and muscled forearms, and he moves with an athletic grace, opening up the umbrella as he saunters across the walk and to the front door.

"Ward Carlisle is who you're trying to impress?"

"Don't look so shocked," I say primly. "He's super cute."

"He is an unapologetic asshole."

"Eh." I shrug one shoulder, and Tilly's jaw drops.

"He's been nothing but rude to me—"

"Oh, please, Tilly. You haven't been an angel to him, either."

She huffs. "I have my reasons for what I've done."

A knock raps against the door, and lightning streaks across the sky in the next instant, followed quickly but a boom of thunder.

I rush to the door, not wanting to get soaked, leaving Tilly gaping after me. She's likely full of questions she can't seem to get out.

"Tara," Ward rumbles as I open the door. God, I like the way he says my name. Like he's savoring it. "You look beautiful."

I lift one shoulder and bat my eyelashes, pretending like I didn't just nearly have a clothes-related meltdown less than five minutes ago. "Who, me?" I laugh, playing off the compliment.

Honestly, though?

It means the world, and I know, deep down in my heart, that's the response I wanted to get from him.

I want him to think I'm beautiful.

I want him to laugh at me; I want him to like him.

I might be developing a little crush on Ward Carlisle.

12

Ward

I've never had trouble concentrating on a task at hand. Never, that is, until now.

Driving into town with a woman in the passenger seat should be no problem. None, nada, zilch.

Driving into downtown New Hopewell with Tara in the seat next to me should be against the law, because I'm completely distracted by her.

The windshield wipers flick back and forth as quickly as they can. The rain is coming down in earnest now, loud and furious, which only serves to amplify the quiet between us.

"Your perfume smells good," I say, then inwardly wince at what a weird compliment that is. Oh, hey, Tara. Just wanted you to know I've been sniffing you.

"Thanks. I can't believe you noticed it. I'm really into indie perfumeries. Did you even know that was a thing? Anyway, there's this little online boutique I adore, and I keep a couple of their small rollers in my purse. Thank goodness, because I lost my collection in the fire..."

Her voice gets smaller as she goes quiet. Sad. Small.

I don't want her to sound like that.

"Tell me about the one you're wearing," I demand. Shit. Overcorrection—I sound like the bossy asshole I am.

"I know what you're doing," she says.

I swallow, glancing sidelong at her. She knows I'm into her? She knows I want to know all the things she likes so I can surprise her with them?

"Yeah, Carlisle, don't act so surprised. You're trying to learn what I like so you can use it on our double date with your ex as proof of how close we are. Smart." She taps her temple.

I force a chuckle. "Right. So, the perfume?"

"Oh, it's my favorite. Here." She sticks her wrist out.

I don't even question it. I just inhale. "I don't know what that is, but I like it."

"Smells so good, right? It's a white musk." She frowns, as if trying to remember. "Oak resin, and I think vanilla and cardamom. It should be too much, right? But it works. I have a hard time with perfume, too, or I used to, because the bases all interact differently with your body chemistry... this is boring, huh?"

"Actually, surprisingly, no. I never knew that about perfume." *And I could listen to you talk about it all day*, I almost add. "I really like how it smells on you."

"Thanks," she says, and I don't have to look at her to know she's smiling. I can hear it in her voice. "That should sound creepy, you know? But I agree. I love how this one smells on me."

"You look as good as that perfume smells," I add.

Wow, Ward, seriously? I have no fucking game.

"Damn. You're laying it on thick," she says. "Out of practice?"

"You caught me."

"All right. Well, now they we've discussed my proclivities for unusual perfumes, we should put together the story of how we met."

"Proclivities?" I arch a brow at her. "Like your proclivities for butt plugs and monster dildos?"

Why did I say that? I meant it as a joke, but hearing it out loud versus texting is... disturbing.

"Excuse me," she says, a shocked laugh bubbling out of her. "I do not have a proclivity for butt plugs. Unless you want to torment Becca and Devon with sordid tales of our so-called sex life."

We both dissolve into laughter, and it amazes me that a comment like that, which should have just completely derailed us into awkwardness, has resulted in both of us laughing like maniacs.

"I *am* the best you've ever had," I remind her.

"Dude, can we just.... It was so weird."

Oh. Maybe I'm the only one who thought that was funny. God dammit, I am so bad at this.

"Oh, I didn't mean to—I was just joking. I'm sorry if I made you uncomfort—"

"No, no, it was funny. It really was." She waves her hand dismissively, and that scent, that delicious scent, wafts through the SUV. "I meant how she... got competitive. About sex and kissing and all that. It was really weird."

Tara's giving me a strange look now.

"What?" I ask, grinning at her.

"I don't want to be rude," she says slowly.

"Ask me anything. This is our time to prepare for a double date from hell, and we're running out of it."

"What did you see in her? I mean, she's pretty, yes, and like... I guess she fits a particular mold of a person."

"I've never heard someone say that about a mold and manage to sound so incredibly insulting."

She tosses her braid over a shoulder. "It's a gift."

"I saw..." I search for the right words, expecting that gut punch of guilt and shame I usually feel when I think about Becca. It never comes. "I saw someone I thought would be the right person for me. I saw someone my parents would approve of, someone who would... I don't know. Help me live the life I thought I wanted."

She regards me silently, her fingers toying with the end of her loose braid. God, Tara is downright stunning. I love her wacky little dress, the way her hair is already defying the braid that's holding on for dear life, the purple peeking through the brown.

"I liked the idea of Becca, of that life," I continue, trying to put it into words. "Until I really got to know her, and by then we were already living together, and she wanted things I couldn't... things I didn't want to give her. The way things ended between us was nasty."

"Nasty?" she prompts.

I sigh. "She said I never showed up for her. I missed some charity events that she was throwing. She was always on the board for different things. Having a social life was more important than anything to her. I've never... I'm not like that. I wanted to give her the life she wanted, so I worked really hard. I missed her events all the time for work. It made us both unhappy. We were wrong for each other anyway. She and her husband—" I don't choke on the word like I thought I might—"they started seeing each other while she still lived with me."

"What?" The word explodes out of her, full of incredulity. "She cheated on you?"

"No, no, we'd broken up."

"She lived with you after you'd broken up?"

"I... it seemed like the right thing to do."

"Wow, no. Absolutely not."

I can't help grinning at the plain disgust in her voice.

"Well, I also thought maybe she would get back together

with me. You know, like we were just... well, not broken up all the way. And then I came home, and Devon was there, and she was kissing him."

I grow quiet, expecting the familiar sense of betrayal to flood me. It doesn't, though. Just a twinge of shame at the memory.

"That was shitty of her."

"It wasn't my favorite. Then I ended up inheriting the old estate here and moved from Atlanta and hoped to never see her again."

"Do you think she showed up on purpose? To mess with you?"

I consider it but shake my head.

"She might not be a great person, and things ended badly between us, but I don't see why she would seek me out. I was just as much at fault in what went wrong in our relationship as she was."

"Can I ask you something?" She shifts in her seat, turning to face me as much as she can.

"Haven't you already been?"

"Yep."

"Go ahead," I say, unable to keep the smile off my face at her answer.

"Why do you care what she thinks? Why did you want to do"—she flicks her hand between us—"this?"

I sigh. "I panicked. It was like all those bad memories of the end came rushing back. All the things she said to me in the heat of the moment, and the things my mom said when I moved here, and I just... I wanted to prove her wrong." I take a long moment to look at Tara. "I am capable of love."

Her skeptical expression softens, and something like sympathy and understanding lights her gaze.

"Right, then. Okay. Game time," she says, rubbing her hands together as I pull off the highway and onto the exit for downtown New Hopewell. "We met at my aunt's house. We're going to play up the old Texas money angle, historic renovations, all that. You like gardening, right?"

"I tried to," I say, snorting.

"Perfect. You tried to garden, and it wasn't going great, so I started helping you design your yard. We put in a tea garden."

"You know how to do that?"

"Sure. It's not hard. You just have to know what grows well around here."

"I've been trying to do that for years. Everything dies."

"Native plants, dude. It will change your life."

"Are the tea garden plants native?" I ask, trying to figure out the angle she's spinning.

"No, of course not. We got all sweaty together, installing a... what's it called? The water..." She runs her hands over an imaginary surface.

"Sprinklers?" I hazard a guess.

"Nope." She mimes rainfall.

"Irrigation."

"That's it. Wow, that was, like, the worst possible game of charades ever. Okay, so we installed an irrigation system for your tea garden. I advised you to plant natives. And we fell in love when I hit a pipe and got drenched." She pumps her fist, her face triumphant.

"You want me to tell Becca I fell in love with you in a private wet T-shirt contest," I sum up.

"Ugh." She huffs a reluctant laugh. "That wasn't as good as I thought it was, huh?"

"Nah, it's believable. I think I'd have a hard time resisting you dripping wet in my garden. I like it."

Her eyes grow wide with surprise, and I realize what I've said a moment too late.

Tara clears her throat, and I pull onto Main Street, the silence thick between us.

"God, it's worse seeing it now," she says.

I follow her gaze, and her seemingly random comment makes perfect sense.

"That's where your store was?" I ask, mostly because I have to say something. It's obvious that's where it was—a burnt-out husk blackens the town square, and I vaguely remember what it used to look like.

"My whole life was tied up in that place. My home. My store. Everything I thought I wanted." She traces the outline of one of the pumpkins on her dress, her brown eyes welling with tears.

"Thought you wanted?" I ask gently. I hate seeing her upset, but I hate not knowing what she means by that even more. I want to understand what makes her tick, what makes her so different—I want to understand why *I* feel differently about *her*.

"Oh, I don't know. *I don't know.*" She throws her hands in the air, frustration evident in every facet of her being. "I thought I liked it, you know? But I was barely making ends meet. I thought, at first, that it was because you know, a witchy-ish storefront in the Bible Belt was a real bad choice, but I had plenty of people stop by my booth last weekend. I don't know what I was doing wrong, but I do know I wake up in the morning, and I'm not dreading another day of trying to make that place work." She gnaws her lip. "I just... I thought that place was my future, you know? I thought it was going to be okay, that I would figure it out and it would... I don't know, not take off, but at least be successful."

"Has your insurance company gotten back to you?" I ask, feeling for her. Leaving the city and working remotely has done wonders for my own mental health. "I can't imagine living where I worked," I add thoughtfully.

"You're going to judge me," she says slowly, a resigned expression pinching her pretty lips.

"Why would I do that?"

"I haven't followed up with insurance yet." She rubs her arms like she's cold, peering at me like she's waiting for a reprimand.

"Didn't it happen last week?" I ask, frowning as I turn the wheel into the downtown parking lot. "You've had your hands full with figuring out your next move, helping your aunt..." I grimace, craning my neck as I search for a spot. "And with me. And... whatever it is that's happening, uh, at night."

I can't quite bring myself to say the *g* word. I've never been one to go in on anything that couldn't be explained by science... but I also know what I saw. Saw after many sleepless nights, sure, but since Tara saw it too?

It's a little coincidental.

I don't believe in coincidences, either.

I glance at Tara once I get the car parked. "You okay?"

"Yeah, I just—You can be really nice, you know?" She gives me a small smile. "When you're not telling me to go fuck myself."

"Nah," I tell her. "I'm not nice. I'm not an asshole, either, though. Not full time, anyway. If you want help with insurance, let me know. I work with underwriters a lot for my job, and I'm happy to pull strings or help you figure out whatever paperwork you need to do."

She blinks in surprise. And frankly, I've caught myself off guard, too.

"You mean that?" Disbelief colors the question, and she twists her purse strap in her hands.

"Yeah, I do."

"Why?"

"You need help, and this is one thing I know how to do. Relationships?" I blow out a breath, staring out the windshield at the pouring rain. "I don't know why I panicked and decided you had to fake being my girlfriend, but now we're invested, right? I'm not going to back out now. I'm not great with people.

Just ask your aunt. Or, you know, remember back to all the times I was rude to you over the past few days. But this? Helping you out with some of the red tape so you can get back on your feet? That's easy. I can do that."

She gives me a watery smile, and I grunt. For some reason, it makes her laugh, and she wipes her eyes, grinning at me.

"I know you don't think you're nice, but you're wrong. Now, let's go lie our asses off."

"Not all the way off, I hope," I tell her sincerely. "I like my ass."

"I like it, too." She waggles her eyebrows. "I might have to pinch it again to get into character."

My reaction to that threat is immediate and fierce.

Desire rushes through me, and I realize the truth of why I want to help Tara out, help her get her business back, or at least, get the funds to figure out what she wants to do next.

She thinks I'm nice because I like her. I want her to think that.

And I desperately, desperately want her to like me back.

I clear my throat and arch an eyebrow. "I already told you what's going to happen if you keep rubbing my ass."

"Is that a promise or a threat?" she asks, returning my eyebrow raise with both of hers.

Double or nothing.

"Both." I grin at her, leaning close. That perfume caresses my senses, driving me wild. "Or, better yet, we could get into character by kissing again."

"Mmm, I did forget what it was like," she says softly.

God, I want to taste her lips again. I want more than what we already did.

"I can help you with that, too," I say. And then I throw caution to the wind and snake my hand around the back of her neck, pulling her face to mine. "You smell so good," I murmur.

I don't kiss her mouth, though. Not at first. She gasps as I trace my lips over the delicate skin of her neck. "If you were really my girlfriend, I'd kiss you like this." I press kiss after kiss to her jawline, and each soft exhalation of her breath makes me feel more and more out of control. Each little noise she makes as I pull her toward me makes me want her more.

"If you were really my girlfriend, I'd turn this car around and we would miss this stupid double date, because I'd be too busy kissing you." I kiss her cheekbones, her nose, obsessed with the way she's melting into my grip. "If you were really my girlfriend, I'd give you exactly what you told her I already had."

Her eyes fly open, and a sly smile spreads across her face. "Is that right?"

"I'm not done," I tell her. Then I claim her mouth, and it's everything I remembered and more. She tastes like fall, somehow. Like the promise of rain and cooler weather. Like mist curling around pine trees. Like black cats and magic.

She tastes like something that could be. Something just out of reach and all I want.

"Well." She finally pulls back, her lips swollen. "That was a, uh, really nice reminder." Her eyes are half-lidded, and her breath is coming fast. "We're going to be late for our cursed double date."

"Excellent. We'll tell them we were making out in my car."

She laughs, grinning widely up at me, no pretense in it at all. "Good, good. All part of the plan."

"All part of the plan," I agree.

It's true, too—except it's not the plan where I make my ex think I've moved on.

I have a new plan: to actually move on... with Tara.

13

Tara

The Salt Circle is relatively new to New Hopewell, and like Emma's hotel, it's brought fresh life and an economic boost that's had a positive ripple effect on the entire area. As soon as we walk in, I blink in surprise at the change the brewery's been through in the name of the fall festival. Gorgeous autumnal floral arrangements bloom from pumpkins on every table, and the lighting is low and romantic. Garlands that match the glittering leaves at Em's fall festival are draped across the walls and the bar. And despite it being a rainy weekday, the place is packed.

"Wow," I say out loud.

"Is it always like this?" Ward asks. His mouth is a tight line of discomfort, and it makes my heart ache a little to see how out of place he feels around others.

"No, not really. I mean, it can get busy on the weekends, but—"

"It's because of Em's success at the hotel for the fall festival," a male voice says from behind us, and we turn around at once. "Tara, it's good to see you. Em said people have been raving about your booth at the festival."

"Oh, that's great," I say, folding him into a hug.

When I pull away, Ward's scowling at me. Oh. Oops.

"Hey, Jack. This is Ward Carlisle. Ward, this is Jack—he owns the Salt Circle, and he's Emma's boyfriend. You know, my friend who owns the hotel?"

"Nice to meet you," Ward says, relief clear on his face.

Wow. He's really taking this fake boyfriend thing seriously.

"You too," Jack says.

"You've relaxed a lot since the last time I saw you," I tell him, slightly surprised at how happy and carefree he seems.

"Well, it has been a few months," Jack says meaningfully, and I wrinkle my nose at the call-out.

"Yeah, well, I don't have work holding me back anymore," I tell him.

Jack winces, and Ward's large hand presses against the small of my back.

"I'm so sorry for what happened," Jack says, and I make myself smile.

"It'll be okay. I'm like a cat. I'll land on my feet."

"Plus, she has me to help her out," Ward says, and even though we just talked about him helping me in the car, it surprises me to hear him say it.

It makes him sound like he's... actually my boyfriend.

Not faking it just for his mean ex.

Not faking it just for her to take back stories of how great Ward is doing here.

But like he actually cares about me

My heart flutters.

"Thank you," I tell him, turning and squeezing his wrist. He leans down, his lips brushing the shell of my ear. A shiver of pure need goes down my spine, and an ache begins between my legs.

"I'm not such a bad fake boyfriend, am I?" he asks, and on impulse, or maybe because I don't want it to be fake, and maybe I liked our stupid little practice kiss in the car—

I kiss him again.

And I mean it this time. I loop my arms around the back of his head and tug him down, catching the scent of pine in his aftershave, the scent of rain on his skin, and coffee still on his breath. And I keep kissing him, loving the slide of his mouth on mine.

His tongue against my tongue.

His hands on my ass.

"Well, you two just can't keep your hands off each other, can you?" Becca calls out, making her way through the crowd. The dim lights make her champagne blond hair shimmer.

Becca's voice is worse than a bucket of ice water.

I grab Ward's hands, pulling them around my waist and turning so he's cuddling my back.

And I feel something deliciously hard through the corduroy dress. Something that makes me melt.

Damn.

Good for me.

The goofy grin on my face isn't fake at all.

"Can you blame me?" I bat my eyelashes at her.

"You have lipstick on your chin," she tells me.

I didn't put on lipstick this morning, so I just smile harder at her. "No, that's probably a hickey from making out in the car. Sorry we were late."

"I can't wait to tell Em about this," I hear Jack mutter. Becca doesn't even blink, though, so she must not have heard a thing, thank goodness. "You two must be the couple Tara's meeting. I'll show you to your reserved table. Only the best in the house for Em's best friend."

"Aw, thanks, Jack."

"I guess it's nice being a big fish in a tiny pond," Becca simpers at me, so sugary fake I'm surprised her teeth aren't rotting right out of her jaw.

"It sure is. Nothing better than small-town living with people who really care about you," I snipe back. Oh, she thinks she can out passive-aggressive me?

My mother is the queen of passive-aggressive.

"Ward's told me all about your amazing group of friends in Atlanta," I lie, grinning broadly at her. "And how Devon was there for you after the breakup. You're so lucky."

Her cheeks turn a shade redder, and a teeny tiny sliver of guilt cuts through me, aching like a splinter. It didn't make me feel good to stoop to her level.

How disappointing.

I don't like being mean. But I also don't like Becca. Not one bit. I frown.

What would Tilly do?

Tilly would be embarrassed by the way I'm treating her. Sure, Tilly can be underhanded, but... she wouldn't like this.

"I'm glad you came to New Hopewell," I tell her, and Ward squeezes my hand as we make our way through the crowd of people.

I'm surprised to find I mean it.

Putting up with Becca is worth it, because Ward kissed me. My own cheeks warm.

Maybe I should play nice. Maybe I should just be me.

And just like that, all my trepidation and nerves fall away. I don't care what Becca thinks of me. I don't care about Becca at all.

But I do... I think I do care about what Ward thinks.

So I set about making Tilly—and myself—proud.

"How did you and Devon meet?"

Becca blinks at me, clearly surprised I'm asking something

genuine, and from the look on the men's faces, they're likewise surprised.

Well, that makes four of us.

"We met at work." She tosses her hair, clearly regaining her equilibrium. "What about you two?"

"Tara has the magic touch in the garden," Ward tells her.

"Yeah, that's her whole schtick, from what I've seen."

I bite back a bitchy response, because she's not wrong. It has been a schtick.

Ward's forehead creases as he frowns. "She's—"

"It's really funny, actually," I interrupt, grinning at him. He squeezes my hand, and we take our places around a small dark hardwood table. Four pretty tasting menus printed on flower-flecked recycled paper and vellum are laid out at each seat. "So, Ward has all this acreage, and all these grand plans to land-scape the whole thing, which, by the way, is mostly lawn at this point, right? Well, he keeps planting flower after flower, vegetable after vegetable—"

"I didn't know you even liked gardening." Becca's tone is slightly hurt, and Ward's frown deepens.

"I don't like gardening," Devon pipes up. "Why work in the yard when I can pay someone to do it?"

Ugh.

"Hi, welcome to the Salt Circle." A waitress I don't recognize greets us, pointing to the tasting menus on the table. "Today we're serving an assortment of fall-themed ciders. You can pick from three different flights, the fruit of which are sourced from orchards all around Texas. We also have a small menu of appe-tizers provided by the Plated Pig food truck." She produces a pitcher of ice water and pours us each a glass. "Do you have any questions about the tasting menu?"

"Not yet," Becca tells her sharply, and the waitress falters.

"Can you give us a minute on that?" I ask her sweetly. "But

I'd like to go ahead and order one of each of the appetizers from the food truck, please."

The waitress shoots me a real smile and nods, practically sprinting away from the table.

Ward's glaring at Becca, and I'm starting to think this was a really bad idea.

"I spoke to your mother last night, Ward." Becca feigns serious interest in her menu, and Devon sighs in resignation.

"You know, I think it's so sweet that you still speak to his mom," I tell her. "That's such a cool thing."

"Oh, they don't speak," Devon tells me. "Not like she's making it seem. Becca likes to stay on her good side because Ward's mom is big in a lot of the philanthropic causes she's into."

"Devon, that's not true. I love Erica."

"My mom is great," Ward says carefully.

Devon's so getting yelled at later.

"You know what's strange, Ward? She said you'd never mentioned her. Not once." Becca tilts her head at me, beyond pleased with her detective work.

Shit.

Shit, shit, shit.

"Becca, I haven't spoken to my mom in months. Did she tell you that, too?"

Becca falters, and I put my hand on Ward's wrist, feeling something like kinship with him.

"I don't talk to my mom very often either," I tell him quietly, squeezing his forearm. I squeeze it again for good measure, because he's looking very displeased with this entire situation. I can't say I blame him.

"So you're keeping Ward from talking to his mom?" she asks.

Calm down, Regina fucking George.

Oh, I want to say it so badly. But instead, I take a long look down at my menu.

"I think I'm going to do the sours," I finally say.

"Why would you say that?" Ward asks her quietly.

"Because there's got to be a reason you haven't spoken to her. It seems a little suspect that she walks into your life and you're in love and then you stop talking to your mom." She narrows her eyes at him, jaw clenched so tight I'm worried we'll have to call an emergency dentist for her.

Devon pulls out his phone with a sigh and starts scrolling.

Blessedly, the waitress shows back up.

"I'll have the sour flight," I tell her.

"Me too," Ward says.

"Do you have any IPAs on tap?" Devon asks.

Becca glances down at her menu, still fuming. It's so damned uncomfortable. The waitress rattles off a few IPAs, and Devon decides on one.

"I'll take the sparkling flight," Becca finally pipes up.

The waitress leaves with the order, but she must be picking up the vibe from our table, because she keeps shooting me worried looks. I give her a thumbs-up, and she relaxes slightly.

The last thing I need is Becca driving the overworked waitress to tears.

Another waiter plops the food down in front of us—six small cutting boards laden with all kinds of appetizers.

"Wait, what did I order?" I ask, completely bemused.

The waiter laughs and takes pity on me.

"Fried goat cheese with mango chutney." He points at each item. "Charcuterie with locally sourced artisan meats and cheeses, bone marrow and micro-greens, mushrooms three ways, mountain oysters, and a fruit and yogurt plate."

"Mountain oysters," I repeat, slightly astonished, just as Becca reaches for one.

"Wait," I tell her, holding up a hand. "Don't—"

"Mmm." She chews thoughtfully.

I can't look away. Dear god. I tried to warn her.

"A little chewy. Doesn't taste like any oyster I've ever had."

I stare.

"Devon, you should try one," she tells her husband, who reaches for one.

"Mountain oysters are bull's balls," Ward says plainly.

I grab his upper thigh, trying my hardest not to laugh.

"No, they're not. The man said they're oysters. Mountain oysters."

"You know what?" I manage, putting some mushrooms on my plate. "You're absolutely right. That's what he said."

"Do you want to try some?" Ward asks me, completely straight faced.

That's all it takes for me to completely lose it, and when our flights of cider show up seconds later, I chug the first two sours as fast as I can.

"Good?" Ward asks me, laughter in his eyes.

"Sour," I manage. "Very sour." I barely hold in a burp, pressing my napkin against my mouth.

"That is so unladylike," Becca tells me, cutting into her second mountain oyster.

"Yes, thank you for the tip. You're right. It would be better if I was eating cow testicle."

"Bull," Devon corrects. "Cows are female."

"Wait, really? I thought cow was gender neutral." I tilt my head, the alcohol taking effect. I guess that's what you get when you're a lightweight and chug two without more than a mushroom in your stomach.

Ward coughs, and it sounds suspiciously like a laugh.

"Are we really talking about cows right now?" Becca asks. "They're oysters. You are so juvenile."

"It's definitely more fun to be immature," I agree.

Sour cider number three goes down the hatch.

Ward watches me, amusement plain on his face, like I'm the funniest thing he's seen in a while.

"I'm not getting the notes of gunpowder," I manage, pointing at the tasting menu. "Can't say I'm mad about that."

"Well, you really have to have taste to enjoy a tasting." Becca smiles at me.

Did I seriously decide to be the bigger person?

Fuck that. I put my empty cider glass down slowly on the notched board, trying to figure out what to say to Becca.

"My corduroy pumpkin jumper and vintage Docs care to disagree, thank you very much, outlet J. Crew—"

"You know what, love?" Ward says suddenly, his hand on my face distracting me from Becca. "I think we've had enough. Haven't we?"

"You haven't even finished your first one."

"And that's plenty for noon. You two enjoy your time here. I'll pay at the bar. Come on, Tara."

With that, he's pulling me gently up from the table by my elbow.

I fall silent.

Shit, I really messed up. I ruined the plan. I drank too much, too fast, and I abandoned all sense. And not only did I take the rotten bait Becca was fishing with, I took the whole damn pole.

"They're going to need a bigger boat," I say miserably, allowing Ward to pull me toward the bar.

"Did you just quote *Jaws*?"

I nod sadly.

Ward tilts his head back and laughs.

I listen as he taps out, surprised when he adds a growler of my favorite sour cherry. He must be furious with me.

I would be furious with me. Hell, I *am* furious with me.

I'm embarrassed, too.

I embarrassed myself, and I embarrassed Ward, and by the

time he gets me out of the brewery and into the still-raining air, I want to cry.

"What's wrong?" he asks, slowly opening up the umbrella and holding it over me with one hand, growler in the other hand.

"I am so sorry, Ward. I ruined it. I was trying so hard to be nice, but I just... I can't fake it. I'm not good at faking it. I tried to be the bigger person. But she's just... she's mean, Ward. She's so mean, and condescending, and—"

He carefully sets the growler down and pulls me into his arms instead. Rain pelts the umbrella, a steady, soothing noise.

I hiccup into his flannel, enjoying his warmth and the sound of his heart against my cheek.

"Sorry," I say. "I hiccupped."

A gentle laugh rolls out of him, and he bends, picking up the growler.

"I'm not mad at you, Tara," he tells me. "I like that you don't fake it. I like that you don't even seem to know how. You know, for someone who calls herself a fraud, I don't think that's true at all."

"And for someone who says he isn't nice, you sure keep saying nice things."

He grins down at me, rain sluicing off the umbrella as it rains harder.

"Come on, let's get out of the rain," he finally says.

When we walk back to his SUV, his arm's around my waist. When he drops me off at the guest house, he walks me to the door under his huge umbrella.

We watch each other for a long moment, the neon eggplant blinking morosely in the grim weather.

"Text me?" he finally asks.

"Dinner?" I ask at the same time. "With Tilly and me? I understand if you don't feel like I've held up my end of the bargain—"

"Dinner would be great." He cocks his head at me, a half smile brightening up his face. "And why would you say that? Our bargain's barely started. Halloween, right? That's when we're done pretending."

He steps forward, and I hold my breath, staring up at him in delicious anticipation.

When he drops a sweet, careful kiss on my forehead, all I can think is that it doesn't feel like either one of us is faking it at all.

14

ard

T ARA DOESN'T TEXT me again until Friday afternoon, and I don't even see the messages until I wrap up client calls around five.

That doesn't mean I haven't thought about her, though. Nope, I can't get the woman out of my head.

Tara: Still on for dinner tonight? Tilly would have served crow if she could have found one to cook

Tara: Seriously, though, let me know so I can prep food and all that

There's one more text, two hours after the first two.

Tara: If you're backing out on our deal, you won't like the consequences

I snort. I have never, not once in my life, backed out on a deal. Ever.

I tap the messages, sorting out an acceptable reply in my head.

Me: I've never met a consequence I didn't like

Her response is immediate.

Tara: Don't think I don't have you figured out, buddy. One ass pinch is all the consequence it would take

I laugh, leaning back in my office chair, enjoying her sass way too much.

Me: I don't think you could handle the consequences if you tried that again

Tara: You'd be surprised at what I can handle, then

Tara: Are you allergic to anything?

Me: Why, you want to kill me?

Tara: Why would I do that when you're going to give us everything we want already? Poor motive. No, I want to know because I'm trying to figure out what the heck to cook

Me: I can pick something up for the three of us

Tara: Don't be ridiculous, I've been cooking all day

I stare at my phone.

Me: You just said you were figuring out what to cook

Tara: YEAH. And if you're allergic to something, I'm going to have to pivot REAL quick, so tell me NOW

I laugh. This woman. I don't think I've laughed this much in years.

Me: No allergies here, unless you count my aversion to purple- and brown-haired women

A GIF dings in. It's Maury, saying "The lie detector determined that was a lie."

My cheeks ache from smiling.

Tara: You didn't kiss like you had an aversion to me

Me: That was all part of the plan

Tara: Of course it was

Tara: Dinner is in an hour. Don't be late, or I'll make you do the dishes

I blow out a breath, turning my chair around to the big

window in my office that looks out on my meticulously planned garden.

This stupid fake relationship started as a panicked moment when I saw the ex I fervently hoped I'd never see again. Despite spending more time with Becca in the past week and a half than I have in the past couple of years, I have barely spared a thought for her.

I haven't thought about Becca. Not really. Not like I thought I would. No, the only woman occupying my thoughts is Tara.

THE FIRST THOUGHT that pops into my head when I drive up to Tilly's house is that if anything, this is the place that looks fucking haunted. Not my house, not Tilly's oddly named Pussy Palace, but this place.

The second thought—when Tara comes bounding out to the car, a huge smile on her face and a plaid skirt flapping around her legs—is that it shouldn't be so easy to smile back at her.

I don't think I'm pretending with her anymore.

I haven't been. Not since I kissed her.

"What do you think?" she asks as I get out of the car. "Cool house, right?"

"Nathaniel Hawthorne would've loved this place. Edgar Allan Poe would be peeling up your aunt's floorboards. Mary Shelley would feel right at home with this monster of a place."

She blinks at me, then rolls her eyes, a surprised laugh barking out. "Are you done?"

"That depends. Do you have a wine cellar and maybe some bricks and mortar? A rare vintage of Amontillado?"

Tara shivers, wrinkling her nose. "I always hated that story. I read it for the first time during my senior year of high school at

8:15 a.m., and really, I can only think of a few worse ways to start your day."

"Poe is a genius." I don't care about Poe, not really, but I like hearing Tara talk.

"I didn't say he wasn't. In fact, I think it's pretty, ah, *tell-tale* that the heart of his stories continues to beat so long after his death." She gives me a smug smile after her little joke, and it surprises us both when I snort a laugh.

"That was terrible," I say, shaking my head and holding the front door open for her.

"Wasn't it? It's part of my charm." She pauses in the doorway, so close I catch the scent of her perfume. I inhale deeply, drinking it in. "Terrible jokes and devastatingly good looks," she continues, grinning up at me.

"Can't argue with that," I murmur.

I'm watching her so closely I see the moment my words hit home. Her pupils dilate as her eyes widen in surprise.

"Well, well, well, look what the cat dragged in," Tilly says.

Tara slips through the door, and I make myself smile at her aunt.

"Tilly, it's good to see you again," I tell her.

"Oh, cut the crap, Ward. You hate this," she says.

"Being at dinner with two lovely women? Can't say I mind it at all." Honestly, I'd much prefer if Tilly wasn't, in fact, here, but Tara?

Tara makes me... feel things I didn't think I could anymore.

"You're full of shit," Tilly says, but she's smiling, her eyes twinkling. "But at least he's not telling us to fuck off, so that's an improvement, eh?"

Tara laughs, and when I glance back at Tilly, her grin seems real, too.

"You two are in a really good mood."

"Of course we are. You're giving me what my family's been after for centuries. That strip of land has seen more feuding than the city of Verona." Tilly cackles, clearly beyond pleased with the way things have turned out.

Tara's face falls, and her eyes get huge as she glances from her aunt to me. "What do you mean, feuding?"

"I told you all about this." Tilly grimaces. "Don't tell me you weren't listening."

"How old was I when you told me this, Aunt Tilly?"

"Oh, I don't know. Thirteen, maybe. Give or take a few years."

Tara shoots me an exasperated look, and somewhere in the house, a timer starts ringing.

"Crap, that's the food." Tara throws her hands in the air and runs for the timer, and the kitchen, I presume.

"She's been working on this meal for hours," Tilly tells me, and this time, the smile's been replaced by an expression that reminds me of a raptor homing in on their prey. "What, exactly, is the deal you two struck?"

Her question catches me off guard, and I study the old woman's face for a long moment, trying to decide if she really doesn't know, or if she's up to something.

"I needed her help, and she agreed to give it... in return for the land you want. I get the help I need from her, and you two get the land, and I get to sleep through the night."

"Ah. That explains why you're in a good mood."

I rub my jaw, confused.

"Because you've finally been sleeping well." She nods her head like that makes perfect sense, and it does... but what doesn't make sense is the strange expression on her face. "I wonder if... I wonder."

"Wonder what?" Tara asks, appearing in the doorway.

"Oh, nothing, Tara. Nothing you want to hear about."

Tara's expression echoes my own confusion, but Tilly just smiles at us both. "Does this mean dinner's ready?"

"It is."

"And you brought your lawyer's paperwork on officially ceding the contested land to me?" Tilly asks.

"Can you wait until after we eat until you start that?"

Tilly shrugs. "I mean, I don't see why we have to eat with him if he doesn't want to be here."

Tara frowns at me, and I realize the meaning she's taken from Tilly's words.

"I do want to be here. Maybe not for you, Tilly, but Tara cooked for me, and I would very much like to eat with her."

"There's the asshole I know and love," Tilly says on a laugh. "Right, then. Let's eat. Although, Tara, I don't know why you didn't just warm up one of the casseroles the New Hopewell phone tree brought over."

"Oh, that's an easy one. I wanted to impress you both with my cooking skills." Tara grins at her aunt, but pleasure ripples through me.

She wanted to impress me?

"Besides, Ward cooked for me once, and I thought it was only fair that I return the favor. Come on, let's sit down while it's hot." Tara's dress floats around her body as she leads us into the dining room, which, unlike the rest of the very well-restored and stately home, looks like... a witch's den.

So much so that it's all I can do not to stand and gape.

Florals and herbs hang upside down from the ceiling, and there's a china cabinet full of strange jars with hand-written labels, leather-bound books, and crystal balls. A small tea table in the corner is stacked with illustrated cards and tiny velvet pouches, along with a mortar and pestle.

"I know, right?" Tara follows my gaze.

It's cluttered but not chaotic, the vibe decidedly cozy instead of haphazard.

"I can tell this room's your favorite," I tell Tilly.

"Why? Because it's as crazy as I am?"

"Nah," I shake my head, slightly perturbed that Tilly thinks

I'm such a jerk. "It's full of things I can tell you must love. It's nice. Peaceful."

"*Right.*" Tara stretches the word out long, and both women are staring at me like I've suddenly turned bright green.

"Is he feeling okay?" Tilly asks Tara. "He's being... polite."

"I feel great. Sleep, it turns out, is the answer." *And so's your beautiful niece,* I almost add.

"What's two plus two?" Tilly peers at me.

"Sleep," I say, without missing a beat.

"Right. Well, we better serve him dinner so he can't later claim we starved him to death."

"It's served," Tara says in a sing-song voice, gesturing to a high-backed wooden chair.

Sure enough, there are covered platters all along the table, and flickering taper candles cast warm light through the room.

Tara claps her hands twice, and the overhead lights turn off, leaving the room lit by candlelight.

"Magic," Tilly tells me in a stage whisper.

"The clapper," Tara corrects, grinning at her aunt. "Take a seat, y'all. It's nothing too fancy—"

"Don't do that humble chef shit, Tara," Tilly grumbles. "It's fancy. She cooked it all from scratch. Roast chicken, potatoes au gratin, hand-trimmed French green beans... and I think a black forest cake?"

"Yep." Tara nods. "The cake was a beast. I don't know that I should have bitten that off."

"It sounds incredible," I say, and I mean it.

Even better? She made it *for me.*

This candlelit dinner, home-cooked and laborious, was not part of our fake dating deal.

But she did it anyway—and I've never liked the idea of a roasted chicken more.

15

Tara

The table's silent as we dig into the food—not the awkward silence I was expecting, but the silence of hungry people enjoying what's on the table before them.

I sneak little peeks at Ward between bites of my own, and Tilly keeps looking between us meaningfully.

"This is delicious," Ward says, helping himself to another slice of roasted chicken. "I can't remember the last time someone cooked a meal for me."

"Surely you cook for yourself," Tilly says. "What's the difference?"

"Oh please," I say. "That's rich coming from the woman who conned the entire town into bringing over meals for her poor niece." A snorted laugh comes out, and the corner of Ward's mouth kicks up into a smile.

I'm starting to think I was wrong about him.

Maybe it was that kiss, or the hurt I saw on his face when he saw his ex, or the fact that I just plain like talking to him. When he's slept, at least.

Or maybe it's because I haven't dated anyone in a very long time and Ward's hot, available, and—some of the time—charming.

He couldn't remember the last time someone cooked for him, and I can't remember the last time I had sex.

My cheeks burn, and I swallow too fast, choking on a green bean.

Tilly slaps me across the back, and I cough, dislodging the food.

That just goes to show that thinking about sex and Ward Carlisle in the same sentence is a bad idea.

But... as I eat, my gaze keeps snagging on him.

"That was so good, sweetheart," Aunt Tilly says, reaching for the bottle of white wine chilling in a silver bucket. "Wine?"

"Yes, please," I tell her. "I'm glad you liked it."

She pours me a glass, then raises her eyebrows at Ward.

"Sure, I'll take some. Is it Amontillado?"

I nearly spit my wine out across the table, and he grins at me like he's won some award.

"It's a chardonnay," Aunt Tilly tells him.

I'll have to get her a Poe anthology before Halloween. I bite my cheek, but Ward just keeps grinning, seeming beyond pleased that he's made me laugh.

Which is fucking adorable, dammit.

"Tilly's right; this was delicious. Thank you for cooking for us."

"I enjoyed doing it. It's fun to cook for more than just me. It's nice to have the time to do it, and a big, well-stocked kitchen to take advantage of." I nudge Tilly with my elbow.

"Well, you're welcome to take advantage of my kitchen whenever you want."

"I never really took time to just... enjoy cooking." I frown, swirling the straw-colored wine in my glass. "No, that's not true. I mean, I haven't done that for myself since I started up the tarot and tea shop. It's been so weird to wake up and not have to make that day's kolaches or start the coffee. It's weird not going to sleep with the fridge full of dough proofing."

"You made all the kolaches yourself?" Ward sounds mystified, the candlelight dancing off his strong jaw. "Why not outsource them?"

"*That's what I always said*," Tilly says. "My Tara is incredibly stubborn, though."

I shrug. "It was something I knew I could do for less. Keep overhead down."

Ward quirks an eyebrow at me.

A sigh slips out of me. "Yeah, yeah, at a personal cost, I know."

"I wasn't going to say that." He leans forward, settling his elbows on the table. His shirt pulls tight, highlighting his biceps. Is all that muscle from gardening? I guess it's possible.

"Huh?" I blink.

"I was going to say that you must be very talented to not only run the retail side of the store but also make the kolaches—"

"And the loose-leaf tea," my aunt interrupts. "And don't forget her talent at reading the cards."

Guilt slams into me. "More like at reading people," I mutter.

"No," Tilly says crisply. "That's not true."

"She does seem pretty good at reading people," Ward says, sipping his wine.

"Thank you." I slap my hand on the table. "See? Good at reading *people*."

"No." Tilly shakes her head and tops off her wine, which somehow was already gone. "She is good at reading people. Of course she is. She's my niece and the daughter of my heart."

"Tilly." I reach for her wrist, but she shakes me off.

"No, you start getting sappy on me, and we'll both start crying, and we can't show our weakness in front of the enemy." She's grinning at me, and my chest is tight with love for her.

Ward barks a laugh, shaking his head in disbelief. "Crying isn't a weakness, and I've never been the enemy. Have I been pissed off at you? Yes. But you started it, Tilly."

She sobers, and the candles at the table flicker all at once as the AC kicks on.

At least, I thought the AC kicked on... but the unit's right outside this room, and it's still silent.

"Did it just get colder in here?" I ask quietly.

"It's a very old house, Tara," Tilly says, her voice just as hushed as mine. "Cold spots are... normal."

The candles flicker, and one goes out.

I swallow hard, and warmth and coziness are replaced by a sudden spike of fear.

"I didn't start it." Tilly's somewhat random interjection causes Ward and me to exchange a glance.

"The AC?" I ask, confused. "I can go turn it on—"

"No, don't. Listen to me, you two." Tilly finishes her second glass of wine, then pours herself a third, adding a little to my glass, then Ward's. "I didn't start the feud between our families. And I never meant to drive you out of your good senses, Ward. Although it was fun to see it happen. I'll admit that. It's been a long time since a grown man told me to fuck off."

Ward chuckles, but it's a strangled sound.

"I didn't start the feud," Tilly repeats, "but I wanted to end it. I wanted to put the bad spirits to rest."

The room gets colder, and another candle gutters, then dies.

I swallow hard, clutching my wineglass and draining it.

"Should I relight the—"

"Don't bother." Tilly's voice is a whipcrack across the dim room. "They'll just keep going out."

"You mean the bad spirits between our families, right?" I

ask. I'm fairly sure that's not what she means at all, but a girl can dream.

"Literally and metaphysically," Tilly says, taking another long drink.

"Explain," Ward says, crossing his arms over his chest. "And remember, I've already drawn up the papers with my lawyer to clarify the contested land's ownership, so you're not getting anything out of this by spinning some tale—"

"I'm not spinning anything, Carlisle." Tilly crooks a finger at him. "There's bad blood between us, and it all has to do with that strip of forest. It's cursed."

I want to laugh, but I don't. The sound won't come out.

It should be ridiculous. Absurd.

But Ward and I stay silent, waiting for more as the room grows steadily colder. Goose bumps pebble across my skin, and I tuck my arms tight into my body.

"I know what I saw that night." My own admission surprises me. "I mean, no, I don't know what I actually saw. But I—we— saw something. In the woods between our houses."

"And you didn't tell me about it?" Tilly sounds hurt.

Argh.

"I didn't know what to tell you."

"There was a woman in the woods," Ward interjects. "We were both... out in the woods—"

Tilly holds up a hand. "I am open-minded, but I do not want to hear about your outdoor sexual encounters."

I gape at her. "What?"

"You young people all think you're so sneaky, that you're the first ones to ever lick the cucumber in the garden, but let me tell you this: you're not. Everything you've done, I did decades before you were born. And no, I don't want to hear about it."

"*Tilly*!"

"If he's been planting seeds in your garden box, that's your business. I don't want to hear about how he trapped the beaver at the dinner table."

"Tilly! We aren't having sex."

"Oh, please. I may have bad eyesight, but I can still see. The tension between you two is out of control." Tilly raises her glass at Ward, and some wine sloshes over the side, a liquid exclamation mark.

"Tilly, we're not having sex." Ward is biting his cheeks, and I'm just glad some of the candles blew out because my face feels beet red.

"Oh sure, and I was born yesterday. Why else would you have decided to suddenly hand over that land? Your family has fought tooth and nail to hold on to it for over a century, so what else led to the change of heart?" Tilly's eyes are slightly glazed, and she cracks a yawn. "It's the magic of the Pussy Palace."

"Wait, are you talking about your rental or—you know what? I've heard enough. We were not having sex, Tilly. We made a deal. I pretend to be his girlfriend because his horrible, vile ex-girlfriend is in town, and he wants her to know he's totally over her, that he's a total ten out of ten, and I was more than happy to volunteer, especially when he makes it easy to fake it."

Oh. Oh shit.

I can't even look at him. I should probably move to Canada and learn how to make maple syrup.

"Fine, fine, fine." Tilly pours out the last of the bottle into her glass. "There's no reason to yell. Now tell me about what you saw in the woods and leave the fellatio out of it."

"Jesus Christ." I slam my face into my hands.

"We saw a woman wearing a dress that hasn't been in style in, oh, I don't know, hundreds of years," Ward finally says.

When I glance at him through my fingers, he's blatantly ignoring me and only looking at Tilly.

"She said rest, she wanted to rest, and I think I yelled at her to get off my lawn and go sleep, then."

"It was really foggy. Everything felt, I don't know, unnatural. Weird." I shiver at the memory.

"Fascinating," Tilly says, sipping her wine daintily, pinkie finger out, as though she hasn't chugged nearly the entire bottle. "Did she interrupt you while—"

"Tilly, enough." I give her my most serious frown, and she sighs.

"You don't seem surprised," Ward accuses, leaning back in his chair.

"Why would I be? Why do you think I've had a bunch of wild women traipsing through there singing songs and putting together protection spells? The veil thins as All Hallows' Eve approaches. The spirits who died there are restless. Like she said."

"Wait." I gape at her.

"Close your mouth. If you want to show someone your throat, turn and face Ward."

"Aunt Tilly, stop."

She grins at me, though, and I can't help a reluctant laugh.

"You used your gang of renters as drunk ghostbusters?" Ward finally asks. "Make that make sense—not that there is sense to be made out of this situation."

"You promised to help with the ghosts." I frown at him.

"Did he now?" Tilly touches the side of her nose, staring at the candles spanning the length of the table. "I wonder if it will be enough, especially if you two aren't out there doing it."

"Tilly! *We aren't doing it!*"

"I meant ghostbusting," Tilly says innocently. "Not busting anything else." She pointedly stares at Ward.

He rubs a hand down his face, clearly as annoyed with her as I am.

"Fine. Okay? I am older than I was. My spells never had a

lot of juice. Not the kind I'd need to really charge up protection."

"Like a battery?" Ward, bless him, does seem to want to understand. He's trying to meet her where she is, which is off with the cuckoo for Cocoa Puffs in chocolate cereal-landia.

"Sure. A battery. Well, I wasn't getting anywhere with the ghosts, so I had to think of a way to get fresh blood in that house, charge up the spells I made, and keep the ghosts from doing anything... drastic."

"Right." I pinch the bridge of my nose, then down the rest of my white wine.

"You don't believe me."

"I don't know what to think, Aunt Tilly. I know I saw something, but..."

"I have been telling you stories about the Carlisle family and ours for years. Of course, he doesn't know because his parents left town when he was just a baby. You were very adorable as a baby." She smiles fondly at him.

Ward looks taken aback. "Thank you?"

"Tilly, I don't remember—" I shake my head. "I remember lots of stories, but nothing specific."

"You blocked it all out, just like you block out your gift. A real waste. I would have called on you to do it years ago if I thought you would have."

"Tell us the stories," Ward demands. "You might have told her, but I've never heard of any of this."

Another candle blows out, and a door slams upstairs.

"The rooms aren't really molding," Tilly tells me. "They're haunted. Badly." She shrugs one shoulder. "I can keep the first floor pretty much spirit free, but that's it. I'm out. I thought you'd sleep better over there."

"You should have told me."

"I don't have being evaluated for dementia on my to-do list. You wouldn't have believed me. Not for a minute."

I scrunch my nose. She's not wrong.

"The story?" Ward prompts.

"They don't want me to tell you," she says. "They don't like hearing about it."

Dread pools in my belly, and I scoot my chair closer to the table.

No, not the table. Closer to Ward. I want to be near him.

I'm scared.

"You're scaring me."

"Good," Tilly says. "This isn't a joke, even if you made it one with your work. Even if it was just a means to an end."

I swallow. That hurt.

"This is the shame of our family, Tara," she says. "This gift you have? It's part of the curse. And the reason for it is terrible. Terrible indeed."

A shiver takes me by surprise, and Ward shoots me a concerned look.

"Your great-great-great-great-great... Well, I don't know how many greats, but she would have been an aunt way up on the family tree. She fell in love with a boy on the neighboring property. It was all farmland back then. This house was here, but I don't think yours had been built yet. This isn't a happy story." Tilly sighs. "It's horrible."

I stiffen, and Ward stills too. His jaw twitches as he watches my aunt, wearing a suspicious expression.

"Her name was Alice. There is still a portrait of her upstairs. And she looked... well, she looked a lot like you, Tara. Daintier, though. Finer boned. Dark haired and pale. The young man she fell in love with, your great-great exponential great-uncle Henry or something, I presume, Ward—" She looks at him, and he nods for her to continue.

His hand flexes on the table, and on an impulse, I reach out and grab it.

"The Carlisles weren't rich then, and Alice's father, my

great-something-or-other grandfather, disapproved of the marriage. He was a drunk. A mean one." Her gaze goes distant, and the air grows colder.

I squeeze Ward's hand, and he squeezes it back, running his thumb over the top of it reassuringly.

"He hated the idea of his beloved youngest daughter marrying below her station, and he forbade it. But Alice, despite her daintiness, had a strong will, as many women in our family do, and she planned to meet with Henry on the property so they could run away together. Not just anywhere on the property, either."

"The little strip of forest."

"Probably," Tilly agrees. "The way my mother told me the story... she said that Alice's father was asleep after too much liquor, and she crept out in the dead of night in mid-October to meet with Henry. Except her father woke up. Drunk, he followed her to the forest, where he waited for Henry to show up. When he did, her father flew into a rage. He started to argue with Henry, telling him his daughter was worth ten of him, and he would let them marry over his dead body." Tilly sighs, and her breath condenses in a cloud in front of her.

I don't move. My skin's crawling with an awareness of something... something else in the room with us.

Something slams into the ceiling from the floor above, and I squeak in terror. Ward's fingers are tight on my hand, and I wish he was sitting next to me so I could crawl into his lap.

"It came to blows, with Henry mostly trying to defend himself against his drunken assailant. Alice was beside herself. Distraught. She got between them. Her father hit her, and she fell. His next punch hit Henry."

I cover my mouth, my fingers trembling.

"He died. Hit his head on a rock."

The room grows nearly unbearably cold, and then,

suddenly, the presence is gone. The pressure alleviates, and my heart beats so quickly it makes me slightly nauseous.

"He died, and Alice swore that land would be cursed, that no one in our family would rest until the crime against Henry was made right. And it was cursed. It was. Our families fought over that night and that thirty-acre parcel for decades. Who it belonged to was never recorded properly. And you and I and all the women before us, we can... sense things we shouldn't."

"What happened to Alice?" I don't want to know. I need to know.

"It's horrible." She shivers.

"Tell us," Ward insists.

"She jumped off the roof a week after Henry's funeral."

"Oh, no. Poor Alice. Poor Henry." My eyes are full of tears, and one rolls down Tilly's cheek, too.

She's not done, though. "Her father was never the same. He drank himself to death on the anniversary of her death the next year. They found him in the woods where Henry died, holding a locket with Alice's portrait inside."

Her voice is so quiet now that I have to strain to hear her.

"Our families have been suffering for over a century. Those poor souls, all three of them. Their past has haunted us ever since, and it's been getting worse. I don't know why, but I know I'm outmatched."

"I can't believe I'm saying this, Tilly, but... I think I might actually believe you."

Across the table, Ward is stone-still, but he doesn't deny it, either. He raises one eyebrow at me, as if asking if I'm serious.

I nod at him, and he shrugs.

"How do we help?" he asks, and affection for the big man surges through me.

But Tilly just shakes her head, shrugging. "I don't know. I don't know."

❧

TILLY INSISTS ON DOING DISHES, and I leave her to it while I walk Ward out to his car. I hug my arms around myself. The night air is brisk. Texas is finally giving up and deciding it's time for autumn, after all.

We're both silent, but it's a comfortable quiet, and worth savoring.

Stars are bright overhead, the sky clear above the Piney Woods.

"Can I drive you back to the Pussy Palace?" He cracks a smile, and I grin.

"Sounds so official when you call it that."

"There is nothing unofficial about the Pussy Palace." He nods seriously, and I shove at him, laughing. "Very serious place, the Pussy Palace."

"Can I say something?"

He leans against the hood of the car. "Always."

My voice comes out a whisper. "I'm afraid. I don't want to stay out there alone."

"Come home with me," he says, his voice hoarse. "Stay with me tonight."

"Okay," I agree, my voice small. "Let me tell Tilly good night."

"Hurry," he rasps.

So I do.

16

Ward

Tara's in the passenger seat of my SUV again, so beautiful she hardly seems real. Nothing that happened from the moment I arrived at Tilly's door seemed real.

"Do you want to talk about it?" Tara asks. "You know... what we talked about at dinner?"

The moon's so bright tonight that I can see the fear etched on her face despite the late hour.

"Do you want to?" I hedge.

"No, not right now." She relaxes back into her seat. "I just... I want to forget about all of it. While I can, at least. Hard to forget up at ye old Kitty Castle."

I snort, turning the car up my driveway.

I don't know if it's just me, or if Tara feels the same, but every single cell in my body is alight with anticipation. I'm hyper-aware of her, that delicious perfume on her skin, the way the moonlight plays across her dark hair and smooth skin, the pout of her perfect lips.

"I like you here," I tell her, then hope I haven't spoken too soon.

"In your car?"

"At my house, With me."

"I don't know," she says, and my heart sinks. "I feel like I need to be wearing an air-brushed carnival shirt that says *Pussy Palace* to really be at home."

I bark a laugh, dizzy with relief. She didn't say she didn't want to be here.

God, I want her so badly. It's all I can think about. It's clouding my judgment, my thoughts, my sense. Everything. I clear my throat and turn the engine off, but before I can do anything else, Tara's climbed into my lap, somehow managing to squeeze between the wheel and me.

"Hi," she breathes, tracing her fingers down my cheeks.

"Tara," I say, my voice breaking on her name.

"Yes" is all she says, and then her mouth's on mine, answering all my questions.

I don't know how I manage to get us out of the car while holding on to Tara for dear life as she kisses me like everything depends on it.

I don't know how I manage to get in the house, and up the stairs, and into my bedroom, all with Tara clinging to me, kissing me, driving me out of my mind.

"I want you," I tell her, desperate.

She throws her head back and laughs. "Good. It would be really awkward if I was the only one who wanted to have sex tonight."

Tara grins up at me and slowly begins unfastening the buckles on her plaid skirt.

When it falls to the floor in the puddle, I'm not paying attention to it at all. Because she's not wearing underwear.

"Did you know that I like to put just a drop of perfume on my inner thighs?" She says it so conversationally, so off-handedly, that I blink at her in surprise as I digest that information.

"I should probably see if that's true," I growl. This woman, this woman is going to drive me out of my mind.

"You should," she says, tugging off her shirt and dropping it on top of the skirt.

Tara's naked in front of me, naked on my bed, her nipples hard, so beautiful she hurts to look at.

When she spreads her legs, beckoning me, I don't waste any time.

17

Tara

"Ward," I murmur, my entire body on fire, aching with need. Part of me can't believe I'm doing this, and the rest of me is giddy with it.

He doesn't move, though, just holds my thighs wide apart, gaze transfixed, like he's memorizing every dip and curve of my body.

"I'm so wet," I say, needing him to touch me, desperate for it. For him.

"Fuck," he says. "Look at you. Look how beautiful you are."

"Take off your clothes," I demand. "Let me see you, too."

He gives me a smug grin, tugging his shirt off.

I groan, sitting up and running my hands up and down his chiseled chest. "Is this from gardening?"

"Not hardly," he laughs. "I have a gym downstairs."

"It's a good look," I say casually, arching an eyebrow as I pinch his nipple.

"You're going to pay for that," he growls, a mischievous light in his eyes.

"Oh, is that right? I dare you to make me pay for it."

"You'll pay in orgasms, Tara. So many orgasms that you won't think you can survive."

"And you'll do that thing with your tongue I can't get enough of?"

He's laughing as he kisses me, pushing me back down on the bed, and I expect him to keep making out with me, to keep kissing me—

But he doesn't.

He pulls away, then roughly tugs my legs apart, setting to work on my pussy like a man starving.

"Oh my god, Ward. Oh my god," I moan, writhing against his mouth. He flicks his tongue back and forth along my clit. I'm already so wet.

"You taste so fucking good," he tells me, and I gasp as he thrusts a finger inside me, filling me.

"More," I manage, "I want more."

"Greedy, Tara. Fucking greedy." He pauses, adding a finger, gaze locked on mine. "Listen to how wet you are." Sure enough, his fingers make a sloppy sound as he moves them in and out.

I buck my hips, needing his mouth, his tongue.

But he just slowly fucks me with his fingers, both of us breathing hard, watching each other.

Slowly, he removes his hand from my body, then licks the moisture from his fingers while I pant, dying to come.

"Tell me what you want, Tara," he demands, and I wrap one leg around him, pulling him back toward me.

"I want you to make me come so many times that I think I'm dying."

"Good." He smirks. "I want that, too."

"Oh, *oh*," I moan as he sets to work between my legs, licking and sucking and using his fingers and tongue to drive me absolutely wild. My orgasm is so close, so close—and when he bites the inside of my thigh, finger fucking me hard, I arch off the bed, my first orgasm hitting me hard.

"That's fucking right, baby. Come all over my face."

My legs shake, and I'm lost, lost to Ward Carlisle and his clever tongue and hands, riding the high of my orgasm as I ride his face.

"Holy shit," I breathe, panting.

"How many more before you feel like you might die?" Ward asks lazily. He licks all the way down my slit, and I moan.

"I want you. I want you inside me, Ward. Right now."

"So demanding."

"I need it."

He pulls away. "I promised you a death-defying number of orgasms."

"Ward, if you don't fuck me right now, I'm going to scream." I grit the words out, and he huffs a laugh, raising an eyebrow.

"Will you scream while I fuck you, Tara?" he asks.

"Depends how good you make it," I tell him, feeling saucy.

He slowly gets off the bed, and I sit up, watching avidly as he unbuttons his jeans, then tugs them down, along with his boxer briefs.

"Oh," I say, my eyes round. His dick is... large. Thick.

I wet my lips in anticipation.

He pumps a hand along his length, and precum beads at the tip while I watch.

"Is this what you want?" he asks gruffly. "You want my cock?"

"Yep," I tell him, and he grins.

"Yep?"

"Yep."

"You know, I was kind of expecting you to talk dirty to me."

"If you don't put that big, thick cock inside my pussy right now, I'm going to go get a monster dildo from my aunt's collection and do it myself."

He stares at me for a long moment, then bursts into laughter.

"On second thought, maybe leave the dirty talk to me."

"Works for me, as long as you get that inside me immediately."

He groans, and I lift one leg, holding it up with my hand.

"Fuck, Tara."

"You have a gym; I do yoga on YouTube."

He grins softly at me, pulling a condom out of his nightstand, and I dip my hand between my legs, watching him roll it on. Then finally, *finally*, he's on top of me, his lips on my forehead, brushing kisses against my cheeks, then my mouth, until I'm melting into him.

"Tara." He says my name on an exhale, through gritted teeth, and it sounds like heaven on his lips.

I squirm, trying to get him inside me, wild with need and want and affection for this big man.

He lines up his cock with my entrance, then slowly, tantalizingly pushes inside.

"Oh, fuck," I say, squeezing my eyes shut as he stretches me and a delicious, heady feeling of fullness washes over me.

"That's the idea," he murmurs, and I grin up at him.

When he pushes all the way inside, I'm panting, my fingers digging into his muscled arms.

"Relax, Tara. Relax, love. I've got you. You can take me. You can take it."

He brushes his lips against mine, gently cupping the back of my head with one hand. The other works my nipple, even as he begins to glide in and out of me, setting a delicious rhythm that feels so right. I match his pace, chasing a second orgasm. When I wrap my legs around his waist, pulling him deeper, he groans, moving faster.

"Oh, fuck, I'm so close. I'm so close," I whimper.

"Come for me," he says, demanding as ever. His palm

smooths over my torso, lower, until he's working my clit with his fingers as he pumps in and out. "Come for me, Tara, do it."

"Yes, yes, harder," I manage.

"You want it harder?"

"Please," I moan.

"Fuck, Tara," he murmurs, then: "get on your hands and knees."

I nearly yell as he pulls out of me, but I know, I know he's right. I know it will feel so good—so I do as he asks.

"Wider."

I spread my knees wide, and he fits himself behind me, one arm around my waist and a hand slipping low, finding my clit again with ease, like he's known my body his whole life, like he was made for this.

"Now you'll scream for me," he tells me, and with that, he slams into me, filling me to the hilt.

And I do. I scream. I scream as he pounds into me, his fingers circling my clit, my orgasm hitting me fast and hard, and I'm flying high on it, limp as he continues to fuck me hard. I buck against him, once, twice, and then he's groaning, my name a prayer on his lips as he comes inside me.

"Wow," I say stupidly.

"Yep," he agrees, and we both laugh. He disappears for a second, then comes back with a warm, wet washcloth. My eyes widen as he cleans me up gently, carefully, and then himself. When he's finished, he crawls back into bed beside me.

If I weren't already obsessed with Ward Carlisle, that little thoughtful moment of after-care would have done the trick.

He tugs me into his chest, and I snuggle in, sighing with contentment. "That was—"

"Fucking perfect. Everything I knew it would be." His lips press against my neck, and I snuggle into him, sated and sleepy and effervescent with happiness. "Tara, I..."

"Mmm?" I ask, already half-asleep.

"I really like you. I don't want to fake it. I want it to be real."

"Good," I tell him, yawning. "It is real."

He's silent for so long I think maybe he's fallen asleep on me. "It is?"

"Yeah, you mountain oyster. I'm totally falling in love with you."

He doesn't answer, but when he pulls me even closer, tucking the blankets over my body, I don't care that I've put it all on the line for him.

I wanted him to know he's worthy of love.

18

Ward

She's falling in love with me.

Thank fuck.

Relief and happiness and all the good emotions are flooding my system, and I can't even answer her before she's fallen asleep, her breathing deep and sweet and even.

She's falling in love with me.

I inhale the perfect smell of her skin and hair, savoring the feel of her warm body against mine, and before long, I've drifted off, too.

WE'RE IN THE WOODS. It's cold.

"Ward?" Tara materializes out of nothing next to me, a confused expression on her face. "What's happening?"

"We're dreaming," I tell her, because yeah, obviously that's what's going on.

"Oh, right." She shrugs. "In the woods?"

"Yeah."

"It's cold."

"Yeah." We keep walking for a while, toward what, I don't know. I just know I have to get there, that Tara and I have to get there together.

Pine needles crunch under our feet, and more than once, animal eyes glow at us from the trees.

"I don't like this," Tara mumbles, and I grab her hand, squeezing it.

She's right. The farther into the woods we get, the thicker the mist gets, clinging to us with grasping fingers. My sense of dread increases with every step, the weight of my legs suddenly impossible to bear.

"Can't move," Tara says, her eyes round with terror. "Why does this feel so real?"

There are cobwebs and pine needles in her hair, but when I try to brush them away, my hands are as heavy as my legs.

"Alice, Alice, are you out there?" a young male voice calls, and seconds later, a man with a boyish face enters the clearing, wearing old-fashioned pants.

"Oh no," Tara whispers. "Oh no. This isn't good at all."

The hair on the back of my neck stands up.

"Wake up, wake up, wake up," Tara says. "This isn't good."

"I'm here, Henry." A lovely young woman, nearly the spitting image of Tara, runs into the woods carrying a small bag. Henry catches her up in his arms, spinning her around as she laughs. The sound is so light and carefree and at odds with the thick, tangible feeling of terror.

"Are you sure you want to run away? To marry me?"

Alice nods, a bow in her hair flopping with her enthusiasm. "Yes, Henry, yes. Let's do what we talked about, the handfasting?"

"I want to marry you in a church, like you deserve."

"And I want to marry you now." Alice sticks her chin out, defiant. I've seen the same look on Tara's face more than once.

"How am I supposed to say no to that?"

Alice beams at him and unties the ribbon from her hair, a thick green velvet length.

"Are you ready?" she asks him breathlessly.

It's not easy for them to tie the ribbon around their wrists, and they laugh at each other as they awkwardly manage the velvet.

"Repeat after me," Alice says in a sing-song voice, and a thrum of power goes through the clearing, leaving my ears ringing.

Tara is tense next to me, her mouth open in horror.

"As our hands are bound together, so are our hearts and minds and souls."

Henry repeats the vow, gazing at Alice with such love in his eyes that it hurts.

"We are united in love, trust, and partnership through the knots of this binding—"

"What devilry is this?" A huge man with hair graying at the temples staggers into the clearings. "Alice, you dare defy me?"

"Father, no—"

The figures turn ghostly, their actions speeding up so fast I can hardly see what's happening. My stomach turns, and Tara's practically panting with anxiety next to me.

When the figures flicker back into solid form, Alice is weeping over Henry's body as her father tugs her away.

"*Shit*," Tara breathes, and I try to reach for her again, but I can't move. I want to hold her. I need her.

Suddenly, Alice vanishes from her father's grip, reappearing right in front of us.

I can't breathe.

Where her eyes should be, there's nothing. Nothing.

"Finish the vows. Finish the handfasting. Let us rest."

Henry reappears behind her, one hand on her shoulder, his face gaunt and full of grief.

"*Let us rest.*"

19

Tara

I sit bolt upright, drenched in a cold sweat. The first pale fingers of dawn reach through the window.

"It was a dream," Ward mutters sleepily.

"Wake up," I tell him, feeling sick and on the verge of tears. Nope, scratch that, I am crying.

"I had a nightmare," he says, sitting up and pulling me too him. He's clammy, his skin cold to the touch.

"I did, too," I sob. "It was Alice and Henry—"

"I was in the woods," Ward says at the same time.

He stares at me, white as a sheet, and I know.

I know it wasn't just a dream.

Slowly, he reaches up, tugging something out of my hair. A cobweb-covered pine needle.

My hands start shaking. "Tell me about your dream."

"You were in it," he says slowly. "We saw—"

"We saw Alice's father murder Henry after they handfasted," I finish.

"What the fuck?" Ward asks.

"I don't know."

"Do you remember what she said at the end?"

I shiver. I won't ever forget any of it. Ever. "She said finish it. So they can rest."

"Finish what?"

"The handfasting," I tell him.

"I don't know what that is."

"It's a type of marriage ceremony." I stare at him in desperation, knowing what we need to do to help Alice and Henry—and to stop the damn hauntings—but unwilling to lead him to the conclusion.

"Marriage?" he repeats. "They were marrying each other when…" He sighs unhappily. "This is terrible."

"They were in love, and they had their whole lives stolen from them. I was scared to death in the dream… or whatever it was, but really? Really, I just feel sad for them."

"Well, let's find some rope."

"Huh?" His matter-of-fact statement catches me off guard.

"Yeah, I don't have any velvet ribbon, you know?" he says, one eyebrow raised.

I kiss him impulsively, throwing my arms around his neck, my whole heart in it.

"Are you asking me to marry you?"

"I'm asking you to handfast—is that right?"

I nod.

"Will you handfast me in the woods so we can finally get some sleep?"

"Is that the only reason?" I ask quietly.

"You know it's not," he says stubbornly. "I'm not about to pressure you into anything with me, but if some ghosts make you tie the knot"—understanding dawns on his face—"oh. I get it now."

I can't help a small laugh that trickles out of me.

"Like I was saying, if some ghosts are going to make us get married, who am I to argue with literal spirits?"

"You're taking this all really well," I say mildly.

"Yeah." He scratches his jaw. "You know, I do have one request, though. Before we go get married in secret, that is."

"What's that?" I shove at his arm playfully. "Sex? A blowjob? A monster dildo collection of your own?"

"Move in with me," he says seriously.

I blink.

"Just until you're ready to find your own place, or until you're sick of me, or you know, never move out..." He raises both eyebrows.

"You want me to live with you?"

"We're getting married with ghosts as our witnesses. I think you should move in with me. Just for a little while, you know, and then you can move out." He shrugs a shoulder. "Or maybe you'll become addicted to my scratch pancakes and never leave."

A goofy grin takes over my face. "Ward Carlisle, are you asking me to leave my Pussy Palace?"

"Tara, I'm asking you to let me worship at your pussy palace every night."

I laugh, and then nod. "Yep."

"Yep?"

"Yep."

He jumps out of bed completely naked. "All right, let's go find a rope."

It takes us way longer to find something suitable for our handfasting than either of us planned on, and Ward's insisted I wear a pair of his sweatpants and his sweatshirt out in the woods, so by the time we're walking through the contested property, the sun's fully up.

It's a beautiful October day, and it seems completely at odds with the nightmare from last night.

"It seems weird that it's so sunny and nice," I tell Ward.

"You deserve all the sunshine and perfect fall days," he says immediately, and my heart squeezes with affection for him.

Neither one of us needs help remembering the way, and we fall silent as we walk.

"Do you feel it?" I ask him, squeezing his hand.

"Déjà vu or that something's watching us? Because I feel both."

"Yep," I say immediately, and he laughs, a sound that's quickly cut off by the fact that we're there.

The same clearing we were in last night, dreaming or otherwise.

There's no one else here, no one that we can see, at least, but I can feel them. It's colder this deep in the woods.

"I'm glad you made me wear your sweats."

"I can't wait to take them off you." He spanks my butt, and I squeal in surprise.

"That feels disrespectful," I whisper at him. "They're watching."

"I know," he says. "I can feel it. But I wanted them to see that we're going to have fun being married." He pulls the knot of kitchen twine out of his pocket and holds his hand out, palm up.

I take it, and the solemnity of the occasion hits me.

"We're doing this," I whisper.

"Any regrets?"

I consider his question, and his brow furrows as he waits.

"You know, I feel like I should be more... worried about it. Marrying you, moving in, all that. But... it feels right." What an inadequate way to say it.

"It feels right," he agrees, and when he says it, it doesn't feel inadequate at all.

Together, we wrap the cord around our wrists. I stick my tongue out as we tie it, concentrating.

"This would be easier with someone else tying it for us."

"Yeah, but when it comes down to it, marriage is just between the two of us, isn't it?" He's smiling down at me, so sincere and full of hope that he's all I can see. He's all I want to see.

"Do you remember the vows?" he asks.

"Nope," I shake my head, then tug my phone out of the sweatpants pocket with my free hand. It takes no time at all to pull up the vows on the internet, and Ward strokes the inside of my wrist slowly while he waits.

"Are you sure?" I might as well ask him one last time.

"Tara, I have never been more sure in my life."

"Good." We grin at each other like fools for a minute. "Repeat after me," I tell him, and a shiver goes down my spine.

We're repeating history.

"As our hands are bound together, so are our hearts and minds and souls."

Ward repeats the line, his fingers steady and sure as he holds my wrist. No one has ever looked at me like he's looking at me now. I'm sure of it.

"We are united in love, trust, and partnership through the knots of this binding—" I pause, glancing at my phone, and Ward repeats what I've said.

Cold air rushes past my shoulders, picking up my loose hair and blowing it around.

"May the ties of this handfasting grow stronger with each new challenge and triumph." The words begin to affect me. The reality of what it means to promise to another person to not just marry them, but to live life with them, through thick in thin, hits me hard.

Maybe we've both lost our minds, committing to each other like this after no time at all, but... it feels good. It feels good to make a promise to try, to acknowledge that there's no such thing as easy when it comes to life.

It feels real.

A tear rolls down my cheek, and Ward reaches up with his other hand and knocks it away, repeating the vow.

"May our love be a beacon of hope to those who know us."

Ward repeats it, leaning down so his forehead touches mine.

A breeze rushes through the clearing, rustling the pine trees all around, a susurrus of noise—like the woods are sighing.

Like two souls are finally at rest.

"You think they're gone?" Ward asks.

"I think they're at peace," I say heavily. I'm tired, drained, although all I've done is make a few promises to a man I'm falling in love with more every second.

It's almost like simple words of love and kindness are the most powerful magic of all.

"Come on," Ward tells me, tugging me into his arms. I squeal as he lifts me up.

"You can't carry me the whole way back."

"You're my bride now. I can carry you whenever and however I choose."

"You're just supposed to carry me over the threshold," I complain, laughing.

"Well, I want to carry you farther than most husbands." He plods along, and I settle into his arms. "I plan on being married to you for a very, very long time."

"I thought this whole moving in thing was until I get back on my feet."

"Sure."

I side-eye him.

"Why do you think I'm carrying you?" he asks slyly.

"You are such a dork," I say, laughing.

"Yeah, but you married me."

"Smug."

"Hell yeah, I am." He falls silent for a moment. "You think your aunt will give us her monster dildo collection as a wedding present? I hear their heirloom quality."

My laughter echoes along the pines.

"She probably would. But right now? There's only one thing I'm interested in."

"Oh yeah? Is it my big, hard—"

"Fluffy stack of homemade pancakes," I finish.

"I can do that." He leans down, planting a firm kiss on my lips as we walk.

And he does.

EPILOGUE

Tara

We fake date the rest of the month.

Fake, because we're very much not actually dating.

Not fake as in pretend, though.

Nope, there's no pretending we aren't falling in love. There are definitely worse things than falling in love with your secret husband.

Em's delighted by it, and instead of doubling with Becca and her husband, who cut their honeymoon short and get the hell out of New Hopewell, Jack and Em join us for all the fall-themed fun.

Tonight, though, we're at home, watching old Halloween movies and carving pumpkins.

"It's gross, you know?" I wrinkle my nose, dumping the guts on his butcher paper lined table. "It's so gooey. It's weird to think that people opened these bad boys up and thought, yum, that looks delicious."

Ward grins at me from over his own eviscerated pumpkin. "I'm going to roast the seeds now, just for that comment."

"Spicy?" I ask, raising one eyebrow.

"Do you want them spicy?"

"You know I love the spice."

"I'll do yours spicy and mine sweet, deal?"

"Deal." I frown, staring at the paper pattern of a bat I'm somehow supposed to carve on the lumpy surface. "I don't know if I'm cut out for squash artistry."

"You're not supposed to be cut out for it, it's supposed to be cut out by you," Ward says airily.

I lift a handful of pumpkin guts threateningly. "Don't make me use this."

My phone buzzes, though, and I take the opportunity to abandon my pumpkin and wash up to respond to the message lighting up the screen.

Em: You sure you don't want to come to the haunted corn maze? It's the last night. Come on, it's Halloween!

I nudge Ward, showing him the text, and he laughs loud, just like I knew he would.

Me: I'm all set on hauntings at the moment, thanks, though
Em: FINE

"Good enough," Ward says, and turns his pumpkin around, showing off a very stereotypical smiling Jack O'Lantern.

"Cute." I tell him. "Now do mine."

He laughs, shaking his head but comes around the table. "Let's wait to do this again until we have kids."

I stiffen, my eyes round. "You want kids?"

"I talked to my mom today," he adds carefully.

"That is so not an answer," I say through a laugh. "How was it?"

"She said that Becca is back from her honeymoon, telling tales about my purple-haired girlfriend to anyone who will listen... and what did she call her? Insufferable. She said she can't wait to meet you."

"Oh," I say, hardly breathing as Ward deftly finishes scooping out my pumpkin and promptly begins carving a spooky face on the front. "That's really... nice."

"Yeah. I thought so too. It was a good conversation, actually. I think... I think it will take a while to fix things between us, but talking to her today made me realize it can be fixed."

I tuck my arms around his waist, beyond happy for him. I know things with his mom have been tense since he moved here. "I'm thrilled for you."

"You're making it very hard to cut your pumpkin."

"Sorry," I tell him, then decide to go wash my hands again. Pumpkin guts and skin are two things that really don't mix. "Wait." Frowning, I scrub at my fingernails. "I still don't get what that has to do with kids."

"My mom asked if I was going to marry you." It comes out totally off hand.

"Did you tell her? That we are... kind of married?"

"I told her marriage has been a topic of conversation, and she said she couldn't wait to play with her grandbabies."

I grin as I turn off the faucet. "I see. Presumptuous, but I like a woman who says what she means."

"There," he says, turning the pumpkin so I can see its surprised face.

"Much better than the bat."

"You think?"

"Yeah, because now we're done with squash."

He laughs at that, and we take the pumpkins out front, setting them on the porch, even though we won't get any trick-or-treaters, not all the way out here. The pumpkins are just for us.

And whatever else might be watching.

Once we get the kitchen all clean and pumpkin-free, I make

him snuggle up to me on the couch. Well, *make* is a strong verb, but I definitely monopolize the couch and his lap.

"Pass the candy bucket?" I ask Ward. He doesn't bother; just fishes out two of my favorites—a peanut butter cup and a peppermint patty. "Thanks."

"Of course. I love you."

He blinks at me, clearly surprised at himself. On the TV, three witches sing "I Put A Spell On You" at a crowded costume party.

"Hmm?" I say, nudging him with my foot. A few weeks ago, he brought home cozy pumpkin-patterned socks for me, and I'm wearing them now, as I tap him with my toes. "What's that?"

"I love you," he repeats, grabbing my foot and tickling the arch. "And I love these pumpkin socks, and I love the way you laugh and get breathless when I tickle you, and I love falling asleep with you in my arms every night, and—"

"I love you, too," I tell him, grinning widely.

"I know," he says.

"Agh!"

"What?" He shrugs, passing me another peanut butter cup. "You say it in your sleep."

"*I do not.*" I lob the candy at him, and he catches it neatly.

"You do. And you *love* me."

"I do," I tell him, grinning. Then I tackle him and press kisses all over his scratchy beard, which he's grown out. "I do love you."

A door slams upstairs, and neither of us bats an eye.

We're too busy kissing each other to care.

scan to find me online

ABOUT THE AUTHOR

Brittany writes spicy sports romance with an extra shot of humor.

When Brittany's not writing, she's usually taking her kids to sports practice, keeping them from jumping off things they have no business jumping off of, and daydreaming about going on a date with her husband.

For the latest updates, subscribe to her newsletter or follow her on Instagram and TikTok.

Head to www.brittanykelleywrites.com for more!

ALSO BY BRITTANY KELLEY

Wilmington Football

Against The Clock

Against The Rules

Standalones

Happily Haunted Afters

Misfits & Mistletoe